Sally Emerson attended Oxford University, where she read English and edited the university magazine *Isis*. She won the *Vogue* Talent Contest for writers and worked on New York *Vogue*. She was awarded the *Radio Times* Young Journalist of the Year prize, a Catherine Packenham award, and a *Yorkshire Post* prize for a best first novel *Second Sight*. She was Assistant Editor of *Plays and Players* magazine, and Editor of *Books and Bookmen*. She is married with a son and daughter.

'Written with enormous panache'
Auberon Waugh *Daily Mail*

'A triumph'
Annabel

'Sally Emerson writes with vigour and vitality'
The Northern Echo

'Clever and well-controlled'
Homes and Gardens

'Her dialogue is unerringly sharp'
David Hughes *Mail on Sunday*

'An absorbing supernatural thriller . . . vividly conveyed'
Standard

'Sally Emerson's talent is robust'
Financial Times

Also by Sally Emerson in Abacus:

SALLY EMERSON

Listeners

AN ABACUS BOOK

First published in Great Britain by Michael Joseph Ltd 1983
Published by Methuen London Ltd 1984
Published in Abacus by Sphere Books Ltd 1992

ISBN 0 349 10247 3

Printed in England by Clays Ltd, St Ives plc

Sphere Books Ltd
A Division of
Macdonald & Co (Publishers) Ltd
165 Great Dover Street, London SE1 4YA
A member of Maxwell Macmillan Publishing Corporation

For Peter

And he smote upon the door again a second time;
  'Is there anybody there?' he said.
But no one descended to the Traveller;
  No head from the leaf-fringed sill
Leaned over and looked into his grey eyes,
  Where he stood perplexed and still.
But only a host of phantom listeners
  That dwelt in the lone house then
Stood listening in the quiet of the moonlight
  To that voice from the world of men.

WALTER DE LA MARE

1

The sun bounced off the rooftops, dazzled the drivers of cars, jubilantly sank its rays into the flesh of young girls swinging their shopping bags and their hips along Kensington High Street.

As Jennifer Hamilton marched along the street she made an effort to keep her head up. Her red curls shone in the sunlight, her white cotton dress showed shadows of her body beneath, and her urchin face was thoughtful. Men turned to look at her, not because she was more beautiful than the other sexy, well-turned-out creatures with long legs and lilting walks, but because of her air of vulnerability — an air which disturbed them as they glanced quickly at the small, slim girl with green eyes.

One man, whose wife had just divorced him, wondered where the purposeful girl in the white dress was off to — probably to have lunch with some boyfriend or meet a merry group of friends, he decided mournfully, as he turned down a side street and out of her life for ever.

A young woman who had met Jennifer a few times at the parties of a mutual friend waved at her from across the road, but Jennifer did not see her and the young woman felt cross. That Jennifer Hamilton is getting too big for her boots, she thought, as she struggled onto the tube with her shopping bags suddenly heavy. She too wondered where Jennifer was going — probably to some library to carry out interesting research, or to a lunch, or perhaps she has a lover, curse her. Jennifer Hamilton was one of those awful, competent, successful people who managed their lives perfectly and didn't lose their tube tickets as she had just done. The young woman grappled in her handbag.

Jennifer turned up Kensington Church Street, passing shops crowded with bright sales clothes and busy with people.

Painful thoughts kept bursting into her brain like cowboys into a saloon with guns ablaze. A three-minute blast and she'd be left shaken but, unfortunately, still alive.

Six weeks ago Jennifer's husband, Martin, had left her. He had left her alone in the big house they had bought together, with spare bedrooms for guests and a study for her and a study for him. Now it was just space and memories, memories corrupted by regret and guilt and how things might have been.

It was a family house in a terrace of family houses. Now that Martin had moved out it was the loneliest place she had ever known. She had loved its high ceilings and huge rooms but now they just provided more space for sadness. Shabby, laughing Martin had seeped into the texture of every carpet, every painting, every wall. He belonged in the house. He was part of the house, part of Jennifer, and without him the house was incomplete and Jenny was incomplete. They had bought it intending to live there for the rest of their lives. They had managed only six years. She wished she could get rid of the feeling that it was all her fault.

It's not your fault, they all said, all her friends, you mustn't feel guilty. It was he who left you. But in her heart Jennifer knew she was to blame. The responsibility for a marriage is always with the woman. It is up to her to keep her husband. If the marriage fails, she fails. And she knew she had sinned against the old law that a woman must look after her man. She had pursued her career — teaching history at a girls' school and writing biographies for children — too single-mindedly. She had behaved as any talented, dedicated man would have behaved, and was now being punished for it. At school, at university, at home, she had always been taught to strive for excellence. She had done so, and now she was surrounded only by the gold of her success. Even on sunny days the house was cold.

She had worked hard at her writing and her teaching and now they didn't matter to her one bit; only Martin mattered. Most nights she had worked until three in the morning, often thinking how proud her adolescent self would have been of her dedication. She had fallen asleep in the spare room with her brain still clattering with the noises of the past she sought to recreate in her lives of great and infamous women. Martin, who was a classics don at London University, had never complained. He was always very understanding about her work, about her unwillingness to go out with him in the evenings, about her weekends spent researching Emily Brönte in Haworth, Emma Hamilton in Merton Park, Madame Blavatsky in the odd little occult bookshops of London. Far too understanding, her worldly-wise mother had said suspiciously.

And now she lay awake until three o'clock in the morning afraid: afraid of the future, afraid she was going mad, afraid of the wind rattling the windows, footsteps on the stairs, even the ring of the milkman on a Saturday morning. The bogeymen of her childhood were all over the house whenever it was dark, creeping into the crevices of her brain, making her panic, pressing their faces against the black windows.

Jennifer told herself once again how foolish she'd been to neglect a man she loved so much, a man who had always treated her with respect and kindness. No wonder he had strayed. She pictured him, his shoulders shaking with laughter, a boyish expression of merriment in his dear eyes. 'Cuddles' he used to call me before I grew distant, she thought, looking down at her feet marching along the pavement. And I called him my darling, she remembered, and I put my arms around him when he was sad and once he sulked because I made a fuss over a puppy. But during the last year I drifted away from him, as if down a dark river.

And now I am too far away from anyone, a long way away without moorings. I really am quite lost, she thought, as the sun sparkled on the pavement in front of her, quite lost. Without him I am only half myself and there is darkness all around.

She crossed over Peel Street, rows of dainty cottages, where two friends of Martin lived. She remembered how clever Martin had

11

been at dinners at their house, arguing, discussing, chuckling, drawing out the other guests to talk about their jobs and their fears and their hopes. And what would she say if she met one of those friends now, if sturdy Mary were walking towards her pushing her baby buggy, or if vague, bewildered Stephen walked by with the shopping? Perhaps he would look away, pretend he hadn't seen her, but if he asked her how she was, where she was going, what she was up to, would she tell him? Would she embarrass him and herself by telling the truth?

The leaves of the trees above her rustled in the slight breeze, and she was afraid.

As she continued her journey, passing close by where a friend used to live, she took comfort from familiar things, from the cars driving by, from the dry cleaners and newsagents. Her inner landscape had shifted so much that she needed some outward stability. The red buses trundled past, the traffic lights worked, everything was as it had been at the time when Martin had told her he was having an affair.

Of course, she should have guessed. During the last few weeks leading up to his revelation she had been unusually tense. She lay in bed beside him feeling as though there were a steel rod threaded through her limbs, twisted a little at the neck. At night he moaned and whimpered but when she woke him he said no, he hadn't been having nightmares, no, not at all. He went back to sleep and began to whimper again and her heart went out to his unconscious body, pale and frightened in the night under their thick duvet. The streets were noisy those long nights: a taxi drew up outside, an ambulance soared by in the distance, her body tossed and turned and it didn't know why it couldn't get comfortable, couldn't get to sleep, couldn't soften into the mattress and the pillows. Knees up in foetal position. Head facing the street. Turn round. Stretch out. Body like a steel statue, but the mind uncomfortably still alive, thinking and thinking back to other sleepless nights, to shapes in the corners of childhood rooms, to why she was anxious when she had no apparent reason to be so. If only there were a switch to turn off the

12

brain, she had thought then — and, oh God, she thought it now.

On the day he finally told her, they had been for a drink with Jane and Robert Neville, who had just discovered that Jane was pregnant. In contrast to Martin and Jenny, Jane and Robert could not stop touching. They smooched with their eyes and their voices. They said 'love' and 'darling' and 'honey' and stared at the door when the other went out for a second.

Jennifer envied nice, well-balanced, loving Jane and Robert. They were ambitious in sensible ways. They wanted to do well in their jobs in advertising firms. They wanted to have a happy marriage. They wanted to have children. They wanted to live good, healthy lives, while she ... she didn't know what she wanted. All this longing and yearning for something out of reach, for something to make her life worthwhile, really was a darned nuisance. Robert and Jane were lucky enough to find content doing up their big dilapidated house, scraping off wallpaper, sticking on tiles, painting ceilings. It had a big garden full of tall old trees which cast their branches wide and seemed to be climbing with the laughter of yet unborn children. Robert and Jane looked into each other's eyes and were happy but Jennifer had not considered Martin's love essential to her happiness. She thought she could do without people because she had always been solitary, needing time alone to come back into focus, relying on her work to justify her existence.

Afterwards, at dinner with Martin at his favourite Turkish restaurant, Jennifer had tucked into pitta bread and taramasalata. Martin was so subdued that she assumed the news of Jane's pregnancy had distressed him. He disliked the idea of having children in part, she thought, because children would take attention away from him. Sometimes he seemed a child himself, a vast cuckoo of an infant. She had always thought that this was the secret of their happiness together: that he didn't think of himself as a husband, a male, and she didn't think of herself as a wife, a female; neither wanted to grow up, neither wanted to take on adult roles which would limit them. People admired their sensible, equal friendship.

13

'Don't worry, silly, I'm not suddenly going to become pregnant,' she said. 'I'm in no rush. Twenty-eight is young to have children these days.'

'Jenny,' Martin had said in a begging tone, pulling at his beard. Martin really was a terrible mess. He had a hectic intelligence, a big brown hedge of a beard, unruly hair and hands with dirty fingernails. Although he was of medium build, he took up a great deal of room because he was always restless. He moved around in his seat and waved his hands to illustrate what he was saying. That day, however, he had seemed very much more compact than usual.

'Look, I know you're not keen,' said Jennifer. 'And I quite understand. There isn't the time, anyway. We're both so busy.' She stared into the candle, and felt sad. Something tugged at her, something which whispered to her in the early hours of the morning, or late at night at she worked, something she hadn't felt until recently, a kind of emptiness which demanded to be filled. She knew in her heart it was a desire to have a child but the emptiness made her work harder, in an attempt to subdue these strange, silly, female urges.

'Jenny, I've got something to say, sort of,' said Martin.

'Yes, darling. Can I have some more wine?'

'Jenny, I don't know how to put this, you see.'

'Go on,' she said, with her mouth full and eyes wide. It was not like him to be inarticulate.

The waiter with the buccaneer's black moustache loomed over them, taking away the smeared plates of taramasalata and replacing them with salad and kebabs.

'There you are, my friends,' he boomed. 'And how are you today?'

'Fine,' snapped Martin and the waiter backed away, brushing down his splendid red uniform unhappily. This couple here, they're usually so nice, what have I done? he thought as he returned to the kitchen. The man with the beard is usually so merry, so talkative. He waves his arms around and she listens to him with such devotion and is so pretty. Tonight she looks tired

14

and tense, poor little thing. He resolved to give them extra helpings of Turkish delight.

It was shadowy in the candlelit restaurant. On the walls were murals of Istanbul.

Martin stared down at the red tablecloth and then looked up.

She stretched out her hand to take his. His eyes were bright and black like a frightened bird's.

'The thing is, Jenny, I'm having an affair.'

She put down her glass and all the smile went out of her eyes. She didn't take in his words but she saw the panic. Underneath his flurry of words he was usually so very calm and strong.

'I'm sorry,' he said.

'I don't understand,' she said.

He picked up a red paper napkin and began tearing it to shreds with his pale hands.

'You see, I felt that I had to tell you. I couldn't go on lying to you,' he told her formally.

'That's very good of you,' she said. 'Could you pour me another glass of wine, please?' She was staring at him, expecting his physical form to change before her eyes, altered for ever by this information.

'Who is she?'

'Her name is Annabel. She's an administrator... at, well... at my college. She's a very nice person, honestly.' He looked so nervous that she longed to put her arms round him and comfort him.

'You're making a very bad mistake,' she said gently.

'Look, Jenny, let's face it. We're not really married. You don't cook for me, you don't iron, you don't socialise, you don't behave like other wives. You do nothing but work. Things have gone too far. Of course I know it's my fault too. I let it happen. I indulged you.'

Until the last few weeks he had never complained about her lack of interest in cooking, sewing, etc. She stared at him in astonishment. He suddenly looked rather pleased with himself, as though he had just won an argument.

15

'We love each other,' she said.

'Do we, Jenny?' he asked. 'Are you quite certain it's not just habit, and the house?' He smiled to himself, a self-congratulatory smile. For a moment she hated him and his smugness. He could convince himself of anything which suited him.

'But the house is part of it. It's part of the love.' She leaned towards him, frowning. 'It's because we love each other that we don't need to go out all the time. We're secure. The house represents the love. Could you pour me that glass of wine?'

He took no notice. A far-off expression entered his eyes. He hardly seemed to be aware of her. He seemed already to have moved on.

'I'm sorry, Jennifer. But it is just not true, really. Last night you wouldn't even come to that party of Robert Judge's. I wanted you to come. It was important to me.'

She restrained herself from accusing him of already having asked his new girlfriend to the party when he had casually invited her as if he wanted her to refuse. He had been deliberately putting her in the wrong, she saw now. Keep calm, she told herself. Don't cause a scene. Stay placid. Don't let this anger out. It won't do any good. You know what your temper is like. Keep it in. Her hand gripped her glass tightly as though it were Martin's neck.

'Martin, let's keep things simple,' she said in what was meant to be a cool voice but emerged as a throttled murmur, the first sound of a volcano erupting. 'You've been having an affair with someone for some time, correct?'

He nodded.

'How long, exactly?'

'Just over a year.'

She took a deep breath. 'So my not going to Robert Judge's party is hardly relevant?'

'Jenny, you and I have grown apart. The passion has gone out of our relationship. We're just friends now. I'd like to remain friends.' He said this in a prim, self-important tone.

'We've been together for eight years. Of course the passion has gone. Robert and Jane have only been married six months. That's

16

why they're all over each other. We were too at first, if you remember.'

The far-off expression remained in his eyes and Jennifer began interpreting her feelings over the last months in the light of his affair. For some time he had been distant but she had assumed that he was busy thinking about his work. When he had played music alone in his study she had never dreamt he was thinking besottedly of another woman. In eight years of life together, six of them in marriage, their happiness had been interrupted by many strange moods. She had not considered this latest mood anything to worry about. It was just a stage, she had thought, and no doubt his work was partly responsible, and partly hers. She had been a fool. She had let this happen, just as her father had allowed her mother's affair to happen.

'She's married, unfortunately. But I have decided that we are going to be together.'

Jennifer looked into his lovestruck eyes and her heart went numb. 'You're going to leave me, aren't you?' she said. He nodded. At least there were tears in his eyes. She was grateful for that. How simple things were for Martin: she, Jennifer, was unsatisfactory as a wife and therefore he was changing her. He always saw problems and their solutions with astounding clarity while she, more emotional, less cerebral, saw nothing, knew nothing. Now it seemed to her that she was returning to the blackness and confusion of the time before she met cheerful, sensible Martin.

Apart from his sudden compactness, Martin looked the same as ever. And here they were in the restaurant they had visited so many times. Everything looked normal — and yet it wasn't. Everything had suddenly become very odd and scary indeed. If only he'd chosen somewhere unfamiliar to tell her this news it wouldn't have been quite so terrible. If only he had told her in the spring, when they were on holiday in Portugal. The strangeness of what he was saying wouldn't have crashed so violently against her image of normality. It wouldn't have endangered her sanity so much.

17

She had never suspected Martin of infidelity. She had always assumed that Martin and she would be together and faithful until the end of their lives. And yet . . . the first few times they had met, she had been wary of him. The cool intellect which eventually she had loved was the very thing which had unnerved her. She had been right to be wary of that, as so often she was right on first meeting someone. She had seen in him then what she saw now, a chill which took the edge off all his emotions and made them the playthings of his mind. Jennifer had read somewhere that the easiest person to deceive is the person closest to you, because he or she trusts you. And there was something that made Martin seem very trustworthy. She wondered how many other less serious affairs he'd had, how many times she'd been fooled. He had frequently looked pained and disdainful when she'd asked him why he'd been so late from a party. It had made her feel guilty for questioning him.

She began to eat her kebab because at least *it* was real. It tasted just as it looked, and it looked how it usually looked, and it tasted how it usually tasted.

'Jenny, I'm in love,' he said, as if expecting her to be pleased for him.

She continued to eat.

Had they walked hand in hand, giggled over drinks, stolen morsels from each other's plates? Was their relationship as hers had been with Martin in the beginning, all sex and love and teasing? It was impossibly painful to think about. He had deceived her. She had lost him. He didn't love her any more.

'Jenny, I want to marry her. She loves me. We want to have children.'

She took another mouthful.

She finished her glass of wine.

'Jenny, I'm serious. I do mean it.'

'Martin, you're married to me.'

'We can't go on as we are.'

'Shall we have another bottle?'

'Over the last year you have made no effort. Well, neither of us has. We haven't been a partnership. You've become more and more reclusive.'

'You make it sound as though it's all my fault. It's a great talent of yours,' she said.

Martin's face was drawn but he now had blobs of red on his cheeks, from the heat and the drink, which made him faintly ridiculous, like a clown. Jennifer loved him very much, even then, when he was axing at the very roots of her life. She had watched him grow from a boy into a man, watched his shoulders broaden, his confidence grow, and now he wanted to leave her. For much of their youth they had been close friends; they had admired and loved one another. They had laughed at each other's jokes, formed a united front, grown up together, grown into each other. His practicality and sense of reality had balanced her impracticality and dreaminess. He had liked her wildness and her foolish fancies and dreams of glory. He had seemed to need her — her imagination, her sensitivity, her body — as much as she needed him.

'I think it would be best if we separated,' he said, with that same air of injured innocence.

'Whatever you like,' she said, feeling sick and pushing away her food. 'By the way — what's she like, this woman?'

'Her name is Annabel,' he said sharply.

Jennifer nodded and looked interested. If she showed jealousy or anger, she knew he wouldn't tell her about the girl, and she wanted to know.

'Is she thin or fat?'

'Slim, with shoulder-length light brown hair and a fringe. Are you absolutely sure you want to know this?'

'Yes, I don't mind. I want to know.'

Warming to the theme of his beloved, Martin continued to talk while Jennifer wore a fixed smile. The absolute horror of what was going on hadn't reached her yet. To her, they were still having an ordinary meal together which for some reason had the wrong soundtrack. Part of her was distanced, watching what was happening, feeling that someone else was sitting there smiling, playing her role. And she found it hard to believe that he was talking so enthusiastically about a girl who would replace her.

Annabel was a thirty-year-old administrator, very efficient and good at her job. She came from a wealthy family and was very chic (Jennifer was very unchic — a real ragamuffin, as Martin used to call her affectionately — or had it been critically?). Annabel always had five changes of clothes in the back of her car wrapped in polythene bags (silly bitch, thought Jennifer, with the same agreeable smile). She was married to an architect who never did any architecture because he lived off her and drank too much (she'd probably driven him to it with her endless changes of clothes, thought Jennifer). Annabel was very interested in university politics (unlike me, thought Jennifer miserably). Annabel was also a gourmet who'd always rather have a half-bottle of really good wine than two bottles of plonk (pretentious little tart, decided Jennifer). But at the same time she was very gentle, very . . . kind.

'She wants to look after me,' he said.

Maintaining the same polite, interested expression, Jennifer said, 'She sounds a real pain in the ass.'

Martin pursed his lips. 'I think we should go.'

'You have some coleslaw hanging from your beard,' commented Jennifer.

He stood up, and the waiter scurried forward to give him the bill, looking anxiously at the white-faced girl with the dead eyes.

When they got home it wasn't home any more. It was as though a burglar had been in while they were away and had tampered with everything and then returned it to its proper place. It looked the same but it wasn't the same. Nothing could be the same any more.

They slept apart that night and the next day he moved out, to Annabel's rented flat in Bayswater. Annabel, who had more taste, more time, more domestic skills, than she had. Annabel, whom Jennifer hated. Annabel, who had knocked down all the coloured bricks Jennifer had so neatly built up during the course of her life.

Jennifer said that she loved him and asked him not to go, but he hardly seemed able to hear her while he filled his car — their car — with his possessions before driving away.

After he had gone she wandered down the garden and at the

bottom, under the willow, she discoverd that his pet tortoise had gone too. Oh well, she thought, at least that's a consolation; Annabel will have to put up with pungent old Thomas the tortoise on the balcony of her chic little flat. The thought of Martin turning up at his smart new love's with a tortoise under his arm made Jennifer smile.

The house was lonely, but she phoned up her friends — mostly publishers and fellow teachers — and everyone was sympathetic, and some asked her round. But they were guarded. She knew she talked too much, too wildly, and that they resented the fact that in the past she had been too busy with her work to come to their parties or have lunch with them.

One friend said Martin would be back, another that she was better off without him: 'Face it, Jenny, you were never a couple.' A third reported at length all the ups and downs of her own marriage. They all told her that her sense of impermanence was perfectly normal in the circumstances. They informed her that she was a resilient person and would be herself again in a matter of weeks.

'But how?' she pleaded. 'How do I do it?'

Everybody had answers, the most common one being the word 'time'. Pleading ill-health, Jennifer took off the last week of term. She did not want to break down in front of her pupils.

Those days spent hating Annabel and Martin were comparatively easy. She imagined Annabel's face on a rifle range at a funfair. She shot at it over and over again and once when she'd had enough of that she rang Annabel but as soon as Jennifer gave her name Annabel put down the phone, and Jennifer felt ashamed, a failure, a defeated, abandoned woman. She hadn't even recognised the signs: his nagging, his lack of sexual interest, his late nights.

She composed long letters to Martin and concise ones to problem pages, none of which she sent.

She even missed the wretched tortoise.

It took a few days before the full horror of what had happened flooded in. This next stage was worse. Life began to seem short and foolish, like a suburban cocktail party. She saw black borders everywhere. Nothing had any point because nothing lasted. She'd built up a house, chosen curtains and carpets, had dreams, made a life with her husband — and a very good one, really. And now the structure was being bulldozed and she was falling down and down, freefalling, screaming out sometimes, sometimes laughing, sometimes making polite conversation. But essentially there was suddenly nothing. In time, she supposed, she'd erect another structure and she'd stop falling into this terrible emptiness. The problem was she was so tired. And there was nothing beneath her. Nothing she valued. Nothing she had. Even her books seemed as though they'd been written by someone else.

She received a brief note from Martin informing her he was going away for a few weeks with Annabel to Greece. 'All this has been so draining for her and for me.'

A few days later, for the first time in her life, she considered committing suicide. She so much wanted to stop being tired and afraid. However much sleep she got she still needed more. She was always tired. And all the time she was stalked by grief which crept up and attacked her when she least expected it. It was so exhausting, knowing it was always there, waiting to spring.

She had to remind herself that she was not that kind of person, not the kind who committed suicide. But it was hard for her to know what kind of a person she was now. And at least suicide was a positive, courageous action, she brooded.

She had lost touch with herself, lost Martin, even lost her past. She wished she could remember more of the good times — the sweet moments — of their years together. She looked at old photographs to try to recapture that which could not be recaptured. She tried to find love there, marked with an X. But love had existed in a tone of voice, a look in the eyes — all things so familiar, so ordinary to her, so much what she expected to have for ever, that often she couldn't picture them at all. The love which had pervaded every room, every touch, every laugh, didn't exist any more and because it didn't exist now it seemed as if it had never existed. How ruthlessly the present changes the past, she thought.

They had met during their last year at Cambridge. She remembered the day when she returned to her room and saw Martin standing at her desk, in his grey velvet jacket and faded blue jeans, with his back to her. He swung round. 'Jenny ... I was just ... writing you a note ... I wanted to explain ... why I keep coming round ... I wanted to say ...' Jennifer flung herself into his adoring arms, and that was that. They had fallen in love.

Before meeting Martin she had been restless and unhappy. As in childhood and adolescence, she had felt herself always to be the onlooker — at her mother's dramas, at her friend's parties, even within her own relationships. She had seldom been the initiator of events. She was always observing herself and others from a distance. But, with Martin beside her, she appeared to belong in the world. He was so very well balanced, not prey to emotions as she was. His presence helped her to get on with her work and soothe her fears of death and time. It also stopped her from having intimations which turned out to be right. In adolescence, a medium had told her she had psychic powers. She had done her best to squash them. She did not like being aware of other dimensions. She wanted the world to be as it seemed, as Martin saw it.

To everyone's astonishment, and her mother's chagrin, after university she had settled down with Martin to become a contented machine producing historical data to feed to the girls at school, and clear, well-written biographies. Her angst, her black terrors, her tempers, her desire for other men, her wild elations had more or less gone, although, when she became angry with her pupils, she was transformed into a demon. Once she had slapped very hard two girls who had been tormenting a stupid one. She had not apologised, and they had dared tell no one, although they dreamt at night of those tiger eyes glaring at them from that delicate white oval face, beneath that red curly hair. But her mother claimed that she was so quiet nowadays she was dull, and Jennifer did not argue with her but just smiled pleasantly. She did not mind annoying her infuriating mother in the least.

But now she longed really to be so quiet that she was dull. She hated the noise of grief in her head and the noises of fear outside it. She hated confiding in strangers. She longed to walk through the world without seeing blackness waiting for her at the end of the corridor.

Imagination was a bloody nuisance. She could imagine her own death. She could envisage taking out all those sleeping pills the doctor had given her and eating them one by one until she was slipping into oblivion. She could see herself placing an electric fire in her bath and electrocuting herself. She could even conceive of putting a plastic bag over her head, although, in that case, she knew she wouldn't have the determination to keep it on. She could just about imagine slitting her wrists. She could also imagine what Martin's response would be. She could imagine his guilt. She had to admit that the thought gave her pleasure.

When she sat up in her top-floor study she saw birds black in the blue sky wheeling over the rooftops like vultures.

2

The purpose of Jennifer's journey that day was to come to terms with death, to understand her fear and her longing. The idea of suicide was not so foolish. She could see so much trouble in front of her that sometimes it seemed only sensible to avoid it. She had always been an efficient girl, doing the worst jobs first, and in part her wish for death was a facet of her desire to rid herself of a nagging anxiety that something awful was about to happen.

Also, she couldn't rid herself of her depression. It was always there, at the edge of her mind, like a great black sea threatening to engulf her. Sometimes, when watching television, talking to a friend, working, the tide went out and things didn't seem so bad. But in the silent hours of the morning, when she woke between four and five, or at night when she couldn't sleep, she could feel the blackness lapping all around her.

She wished it were term-time. She longed for the huddled security of the tube in the mornings, when most travellers not only knew where they were going but how many hours they would spend there and what they would be doing during those hours. They were part of that other world, the sensible, practical world of other people. Companionship and the ordinary details of life — the coffee at eleven, the staff luncheon, the bright faces of her pupils, the argument about the character of Sir Thomas More — would have helped to calm her down and stop her from thinking.

She now seemed to have endless space and time to fill as she chose. Martin's breakfast, his demands for dinner, his wish to go to bed, had imposed their routine on her and kept her from losing control. Now Martin's habits and the habit of having Martin

25

around had gone from Jennifer's life and she didn't know what to do with herself. Perfect freedom, she had discovered, is something to be avoided. No wonder the rich were often unhappy. It wasn't the wealth which made them unhappy but the freedom which wealth brings.

She had tried to explain all this to her bald, amiable doctor when she had visited him four times last week, each time with a different complaint, half hoping, she supposed, that there might be a physical cause for her misery.

At the end of the fourth consultation — this time on the pretext of a small spot on the back of her left hand which she hoped might need an operation — Dr Anderson said, 'I don't think there's anything I can do to help you, my dear.' He peered at her over the top of his glasses and tapped his metal desk with the end of a biro. 'But we do have someone here at the health clinic who listens to these sorts of problems. As it happens, she's here tomorrow. Name of Laura. Why don't you come by, at about ten?'

'Well, it can't do any harm,' said Jennifer recklessly.

'Good,' he muttered.

'Who is she? ... I mean what exactly does she do?'

He tapped his biro. 'She's a social worker.'

Oh my God, thought Jennifer, stooping to pick up her handbag, so now I'm one of society's problems. How she wished the doctor would just hand her a prescription to cure her pain: perhaps a love potion — a magic brew to bring Martin back, or at least a spell trapped in a little glass bottle marked 'Death to the Other Woman: open six times a day and wish'.

The next morning Jennifer found she was looking forward to her appointment. She wanted objective advice. She envisaged a spacious office and a woman with a white coat and lace-up shoes. The woman would listen and then, in a few down-to-earth sentences, put her problems in perspective and recommend a solution. The office would be full of light and very clean and brisk.

In fact, her consultation took place in the children's play area of the clinic. Miniature desks and chairs were scattered over a badly

26

stained cork floor. Jennifer sat opposite the grim-faced Laura on a chair made for a child.

Laura asked questions and nodded, a complacent, humourless expression on her pinched face. She wore a tweed skirt and a rather grubby sweater. Her ankles were thick and her nails dirty. Oh dear me, thought Jennifer, this is not what I want, not what I want at all. She is presumptuous and inquisitive, and she makes me feel like a patient in a mental hospital.

Laura asked for the details of Jennifer's problems with her parents, her resentments about her upbringing, her sexual feelings, her inadequacies. All the time she scribbled in her shorthand notebook.

'And was your parents' divorce a great shock to you?'

'No ... Yes ... it was thirteen years ago ... I can't remember.' Jennifer's eyes were caught by a series of wobbly crayon drawings of houses pinned to the wall. She tried to concentrate. 'I suppose I didn't mind all that much because, well, I didn't like my mother all that much. She was always having affairs and causing scenes. She made me angry, and I dislike becoming angry.'

The sun filtered through the narrow window onto the discoloured cork and Jennifer was sad as she looked down at a pink naked doll with its arms stretched beseechingly towards the ceiling. How static everything was: the woman with the beady doll-like eyes; her own upright body, hands clasped on her thighs; the toys in position where they had been discarded — a teddy on his belly, red, green and blue wooden bricks in a row, a few farmyard animals on their sides. Only the light was alive, lapping over the objects, changing them.

'And your father. How is he?'

Jennifer spoke of the aimlessness of her father's life since Sarah, her mother, left him for a younger man. In the years since the divorce Sarah had made a great deal of money running restaurants and hotels. She had spent much of the time abroad. Neither she nor Edward had married again, though they had both come near to it on a number of occasions. Edward had travelled too, writing books about the places he visited, and the prose was

27

somehow much improved by his sense of loss. There had always been something a little drifting about Edward, and the years and the pain had accentuated this quality. Jennifer was aware that Edward was someone who liked feeling sad, otherwise he would have persuaded Sarah back years ago. He was, above all, a melancholy English gentleman, and he enjoyed the role.

Laura's pudding-basin hair weighed her down like a helmet as she examined Jennifer with clinical eyes.

'You know,' said Jennifer, looking down at her nails, which she was surprised to see were bitten, 'I can't even work. I'm a teacher, but in my spare time I write short biographies for children. They sell well. I receive fan mail. People say they are remarkable, and that is what I have always wanted, to achieve something remarkable in my life. But now that he's gone I just don't care about introducing the heroines of the world to eleven- or twelve-year-old girls. I sit in front of the typewriter and think I'll just take five minutes off to think about Martin and how to get him back. Before I know it, I've been sitting there in a jealous rage for an hour and am too exhausted to do anything but have a sleep. If I'm not plotting how to get him back, I'm examining where our relationship went wrong, trying to choose one path through the tangle, one that gives a clear view of the whole forest. But I never seem to find the path and I get so tired looking for it. And sometimes ... sometimes I want to die just to get some rest, and that makes me terrified of dying because I feel so close to it and I can imagine eternity going on and on just as I used to before Martin came along. You see, I never worried about death when he was around.'

'Fear is a normal adult emotion. Do you think you have used Martin to escape adult emotions?' said Laura's nasal voice. She peered at Jennifer as though she were a specimen under a microscope.

'But my emotions now, they're not adult. They're ... they're like being locked up in a cupboard all night long as a child ... '

'I see. And at what age did this occur?' said Laura, turning the page of her notebook, a sudden light in her eyes.

28

'What? No. Of course I haven't ever been locked in a cupboard ... '

At the end of the consultation, instead of telling Jennifer to buck up, that she'd get over it all in time, that every separated couple feels like this, Laura said lugubriously that Jennifer needed 'help'.

'What do you mean?' asked Jennifer.

'We could arrange for you to see a qualified psychiatrist who could help you to sort out your feelings, to understand yourself better.'

'A psychiatrist?' said Jennifer, astonished that she had travelled this far from what she had been, that she had become one of those unstable, self-obsessed people who couldn't cope. She was becoming one of those people whom social workers wrote reports on. She had become one of the people she'd only read about before.

'Oh no,' said Jennifer. 'I don't think that will be necessary. I'm sure things will work themselves out.'

'You said you felt suicidal.'

'Yes, but I'd never do it. Really, I'm not the sort of person to do it. Honestly, I'll be all right. It was just that I wanted someone to talk to, and wondered if you might be able to give me some advice.'

'I think you're making a mistake,' said Laura. 'But do take my phone number, in case you want to talk.'

As Jennifer strode away from the health clinic she resolved not to use the number under any circumstances.

I'll be fine, she had thought to herself. I'll throw myself into my work again. That's the best way out. But in her heart she could see no way out. She wanted Martin back. She wanted her past back. She wanted to be the person she had been, not this nervous, vulnerable, mad woman. How little we know of things until they end.

It was then that she had remembered Mrs Maugham, whom she had met on her first and only visit to the spiritualist church, with her eccentric Aunt Stella. Perhaps if I go there again, the kindly Mrs Maugham might give me some advice, Jennifer had thought. After all, she is supposed to be a marvellous listener.

3

And so it was that on that cloudless day Jennifer Hamilton arrived anxious and confused at her destination and saw again the narrow path of crazy paving which led to the little church, a Victorian building with green, pointed, Gothic doors and stained-glass windows.

On Jennifer's previous visit here Mrs Maugham had given the 'demonstration' of the continual existence of souls. Her Aunt Stella had been a great admirer of the medium, so great that she had bored everyone with accounts of her talents and her willingness to listen to other people's problems. Even her taste for chocolates had won Stella's admiration. 'A superb woman, quite superb,' boomed Stella, her hands on her hips, as if challenging Jennifer to gainsay her.

Wearing headscarf and gloves as usual, Stella had sat bolt upright in her seat, straining to see her heroine as she lumbered onto the platform that day over two years ago, wiping chocolate from around her scarlet lips. The lights were turned down and the medium's thickly made-up face cracked into a frown. The hall had fallen totally silent. Her blue eyes had scanned the room like radar and her vast face had seemed to respond — by squinting or frowning or smiling — to every thought-wave she encountered. Her tightly curled grey hair was plonked on her head like a slightly lopsided wig, which perhaps it was, and her legs were about a foot in circumference, and looked oddly detachable.

The last message of all had been for Stella.

'Donald is calling to you. He says . . . He keeps saying, "It won't be long now." Can you help me with this, Stella? Can you interpret this?' Mrs Maugham's pudgy hands were clasped tightly together above her ample chest, as if from an excess of emotion.

'Why yes, I most certainly can,' said Stella. 'Mrs Maugham, thank you, thank you very much.'

'He's said it again, my dear,' exclaimed Stella's heroine, eyes wide. '"It won't be long now." He's crying out in pleasure, "It won't be long now."'

A fly was bouncing and buzzing against the window and Jennifer could smell the coppery chrysanthemums on the ledge beside her. Mrs Maugham was wiping sweat from her brow with a white handkerchief.

Stella stood up. 'He was a marvellous man,' she announced to the assembled gathering, crossing her arms in front of her decisively. 'One of the very best.'

Jennifer had stared up in astonishment. Stella had loathed her husband. She had never had a good word for him and used to chase him round the house yelling battle-cries whenever he drank too much, which was most of the time.

Mrs Maugham had smiled and the atmosphere lightened as if the curtain had come down on a tragedy leaving the leading lady small, bowing, grateful.

The hall began to buzz with words of admiration for the medium. 'Wonderful woman' ... 'What a presence!' ... 'Shall we see you here next week?' ... 'She's so accurate' ... 'Always the best, I quite agree' ... 'She did so much for dear Matilda before she died.'

Stella had introduced her heroine to Jennifer as Mrs Maugham bustled down the aisle, now transformed into her off-stage persona, a motherly figure with big hips, kind smile and old-fashioned manner.

Within weeks of Stella's message 'from Donald', Jennifer's aunt had had a cardiac arrest and died. Her doctor had been astonished. 'I thought she had the heart of a young woman. I'd have given her another twenty years of troublemaking at the inside.'

Jennifer told no one of the message Stella had received that day, nor about Stella's dependence on Mrs Maugham.

Now, two years later, Jennifer entered again the musty little church hall with its drooping flowers on the tiled windowsills. The ruby and emerald stained-glass windows cast shafts of colour through the dusty air. There was no movement among the people who sat here and there on the dark wooden pews. Each person sat alone, separated from the next by a distance of space and it seemed to Jennifer, as she found her way to a place at the back, that they were separated in time too. Certainly none belonged in the present. They were leftovers from other periods, other places, times perhaps when they were happy: an old lady in pearls and a cashmere twin-set, maybe favoured by the dead person she had come to contact today; a sedate middle-aged woman in a coat with forties-style padded shoulders; a little old man with tufts of hair growing out of his ears and a suit which he must originally have worn a long time ago, when his shoulders were broader, his arms longer. And here they all were gathered together, waiting for comfort, wanting to be told that their loneliness was only temporary, that they would be reunited with those they had loved, that this was not all they had left to look forward to, long hours of emptiness as their bones contracted and they lost even their memories.

A red beret was perched on the head of one old lady, and another woman wore a black beret with a grey fur pompom. How brave they were, thought Jennifer as her heart went out to them all, to all those who suffered in their minds, to all those for whom dark nights of the soul were ordinary consequences, to all those whom others avoided because they were sad. What courage it took, in the face of old age and the pain of life, to plant jaunty hats upon grey, thinning hair.

She noticed some yoghurt on her dress, where she had spilt it at breakfast, and she saw herself forty years older in this same church with other food down her front but the same despair in her heart.

The magic of love is that one thinks it will never end, and the black magic of despair plays the same trick. Just a trick, she told herself, only a trick.

Earlier that morning she had stood at the window of their bedroom, staring out over the gardens.

The windows of buses, of taxis, the windows of houses — she was always the face at the window. She had neither past nor future. She was just a watcher at the edge of time like those listeners of whom her aunt had spoken, those people on the Other Side who watch our struggles here, on the overlit stage, the people who were here today in the church, unseen, waiting to be called on.

Her hope had left her — all the dreams she had lived on — and her memories were fading too. She wished she had kept her memories of Martin polished like best silver but she had always been too busy hankering after the next dream, the next book, preparing for the next exam, to notice the moment as it passed. And now it seemed to her that only memories mattered, a lifetime's deathbed-secret smiles.

Martin had walked off with her past, the past they should have recalled together in old age. Jennifer had some photographs in a few albums, some entries in her diary, and that was all that her life amounted to apart from herself, standing there, by the window, with arms and legs and no internal injuries.

Perhaps the blankness of her memory reflected the greyness of her life with Martin. But how could it have been grey when she felt real with him — not that she could quite recall what feeling real was like any more. She was aware that other people had a solid sense of their three-dimensional existence. They didn't feel that they might easily float up into the air like Mary Poppins at any second. They knew how things were. They knew what life was like.

That morning, she had touched the bedroom curtains and would not have been surprised if they had crumbled beneath her fingers, because she had lost her preconceptions about what happened next in life, what caused what, and what didn't. She was quite at sea, like someone who had come out of prison to a changed reality. Without energy, Jennifer had dressed in the big empty bedroom where she had made love to Martin so many times. She tried to remember what it had been like, and couldn't. Standing still — wearing only her white knickers — she tried to recall

33

Martin's face. And she couldn't. She couldn't even remember Martin's face. She trailed her finger across the window. The face with which she had spent so many thousands of hours. She had kissed it, stroked it, loved it, over all those years and now, just a short time after it had deserted her, she had forgotten it.

Time erodes painful memories but it erodes sweet ones too; little by little everything is taken from us.

Of course Martin and she had had some wonderful holidays, and those she remembered, but she feared she only remembered those because of the grinning snapshots of Martin or her in front of this place or that: in front of Lenin's tomb, sitting on a stone lion in St Mark's Square, waving from a bridge in Amsterdam. Was that all her life was reduced too? All those glorious ambitions, all those moods, those moments of inspiration, that love, those days of wild glee at being alive? All washed away, leaving her just a figure by the window, childless, getting on for thirty.

It seemed to her that she had come to the end before her time. She was no longer the same person she had been. That person and that person's past had died. Now she feared that every few years she would have to re-enter the fire again until, at the end of her life, she would be surrounded by the ghosts of all her dead selves ...

Jennifer joined in the tuneless singing and the prayers to a God in whom she only half believed.

When the medium walked onto the stage she was disappointed. He was not a bit like Mrs Maugham. He wore a leather jacket and a small moustache and looked more like an encyclopaedia salesman than a salesman of eternal life. Where was Mrs Maugham? Why wasn't she here?

The lights went down and a new atmosphere of excitement rose up as the congregation moved in their seats, craned their necks, sat taller, eager for the medium to notice them, to bring back the dead to them, to prove to them that their husbands and wives had not died, only moved onto another plane of existence from where they watched and listened, benevolent, caring, loving. They were like children trying to see a magician, thought Jennifer crossly.

34

The spiv in the leather jacket had a dull voice which became even duller when he failed four times to come up with one name from the dead anyone recognised. He sipped at his water, paced up and down, stared at members of the congregation as though he could see into their most secret thoughts, and came up with messages from those on the Other Side which puzzled everyone.

After a half an hour Jennifer was becoming bored and the church had begun to seem rather an ordinary place. She felt silly sitting there in the semi-darkness noticing a cockroach crawling up the wall.

'Now sir,' the spiv was saying, 'I feel you have a serious problem.'

With mild curiosity, Jennifer looked in the direction in which the spiv was staring. There was something about the way he said 'serious problem' which contained a hint of excitement.

'Yes,' said a man in the front row.

The mood of the church changed. Everyone was listening, looking, quiet, interested again.

'Sorry, could you speak up?'

'Yes, that's right,' said the man.

'It's a personal problem . . . nothing to do with business, is it?'

'Yes.'

'Sorry?'

'I said yes, it is a personal problem.'

I know that voice from somewhere, thought Jennifer.

'Sir, you're looking for contact — for an answer — from someone who passed over . . . a year ago?' the medium was saying.

'Yes. A year yesterday,' said the man.

'She was a lovely girl, with ginger hair?'

'That's right.'

'And an aristocratic face?'

'Yes.'

'You loved her at first?'

'That's right.'

'But . . . she was not what you would call a loving person?'

'No, not at all loving.'

35

'You were often angry with her.'

'I was.'

'Sometimes you were so angry you wanted to kill her.'

'Sometimes.'

'I feel a great coldness about this woman.'

'She was cold.'

'And an emptiness.'

'Yes.'

'But she was very beautiful,' insisted the medium.

'I thought so at first.'

'And she died ... tragically?'

The deep brown walls of the hall were moving closer together, hemming Jennifer in.

'That's right.'

'And the house, where she died, your house, sir, it belonged to someone who came to this church?'

'That is correct.'

'You want to know if this girl forgives you for hating her.'

'I didn't hate her.'

'Sometimes you hated her.'

'Yes, sometimes I hated her,' said the voice less clearly.

A smell of rotting flowers reached Jennifer's nostrils. How dark it was here, and how still everyone was, like waxworks. The cold of the stone floor crept up Jennifer's feet and through her body.

'She says you should ask forgiveness from God, not from her.'

Jennifer could hardly breathe from the dust which was filling her throat and the stench of flowers and stagnant water. She stood up and pushed past the two women in the row; one had a vast white forehead and the other seemed to be wearing a wrinkled mask slashed with red lips. They stank of jumble sales and age and they grunted angrily as she pushed in panic. She hurried out, letting the door bang, into the light of an ordinary August day.

She screamed as she ran straight into a huge fat lady.

'Christ. It's you.'

'Hello, my dear,' said Mrs Maugham.

'I'm sorry. I can't stop,' cried out Jennifer.

36

'My dear. Come and see me tomorrow at noon. Number twenty-three Reynolds Walk, just round the corner. I can see you're in trouble.'

'Thanks, I will. I must go now. Can't stay.'

And Jennifer ran off.

4

'Men — they're so funny — they simply must have you,' said Estelle. 'It's all they want — you. It's imperative they make love to you there and then or, well, they'll die. And then, whoops, it's all over and they're not even sure why you're there, in the bed beside them, taking up so much room. It isn't that they lied to you in the first place. It's just that they're different. We don't want the sex all *that* much — although it's perfectly nice — we want the love afterwards. We make love to win love, and they to lose it.'

After leaving the church Jennifer had at once gone round to her friend Estelle, who as usual had a bottle of wine open, although it was only 11.30 in the morning.

Estelle was a talkative, horse-faced girl with frizzy hair who wore flamboyant clothes with great panache and had a passion for matchmaking. She also loved entertaining. The previous week, at one of Estelle's dinner parties, Jennifer had talked and talked to the man beside her because his interest proved she had some kind of identity. When she stopped talking, she was no one again. Ever since leaving the church, she had been thinking about the dinner party and that man.

She had been emotionally stable for so long — ever since meeting Martin — that her emotional instability interested as well as appalled her. 'Every morning,' she had told the quiet withdrawn man, 'as soon as I wake up, thoughts dash into my mind and stampede around all day until I fall asleep early and exhausted.'

Throughout the dinner, the man, whose name was Richard, had hardly taken his eyes off her, although she had been very boring and self-indulgent. His eyes were interested, amused,

38

inquiring in his static face with its overhanging forehead, grey eyebrows, and sunken cheeks.

As she left, he told her that he knew her from somewhere, but could not remember where.

And now that voice, ringing out in the church . . . she was almost sure it had been his voice, very warm and clear but with an undertow of fear . . .

'My problem is that I like kissing, you know,' continued Estelle, with her head on one side. 'Whenever I see a man who's just a bit attractive, I want to kiss him. And they think that means you want to go to bed with them, and if you don't they think you've been leading them on. It is unfair.' Estelle's South Kensington flat was untidy, covered in paperclips, dirt, half-filled coffee cups and books all over the floor. But she emerged out of it like a butterfly, colourful, full of life, laughing at whatever disaster she had just precipitated from her habits of kissing and matchmaking. She longed to get married but whenever she met anyone suitable she fixed them up with someone else who needed a husband more. Six of her previous lovers had met their wives through her.

'I kissed this man at a party, and before I knew it I was back in his flat being tied up to the bed and made love to five times in one night. I quite enjoyed it but he didn't even take my phone number. And all I had wanted was a little snog. Still, I'm going out with Jonathan tonight and he's impotent so I can just enjoy the foreplay and not have to put up with being smacked or tied up or any of the other awful things men seem to want to do to one nowadays. How are you then? Is Martin crawling back to you on his knees yet?'

'No.'

'Somebody just phoned me for your number, you know.' Estelle delivered Jennifer a sly sidelong glance.

'Who was that?'

'Don't you know?'

'No.'

'I invited him because I thought you two would get on. You're both as serious as each other.'

39

'What do you mean?'

'You take yourself so seriously. Things matter to you. They don't matter so much to me.'

'Who wanted my phone number, Estelle? Don't tease me.'

Jennifer was curled up on Estelle's sofa, hugging a glass in her hand as though it were a comforting mug of drinking chocolate.

'Richard, of course, Richard Stevenson.'

From the wall, a painting of a cat stared at Jennifer and she stared back, both big-eyed, startled, at odds with the easy charm of Estelle.

'You've gone quite pale. What's the matter? Don't you like him?'

Jennifer shook her head. 'It's not that.'

'Have some more wine.'

'Thank you.' Jennifer glanced down at her glass, which was rather dirty. She watched as Estelle poured the blood-red liquid into what was in fact a tumbler for gin. It was chipped in two places.

'I think he's gorgeous.' Estelle pulled up her scarlet tights from the ankles to straighten them, wiggling as she did so. Two matching red combs kept her hair off her long face.

'Why don't you go out with him then?' muttered Jennifer.

'Too serious for me. Too intense and balled up. His first wife died, you know.' Estelle subsided into her bentwood rocking chair, long legs stretched out in front of her.

'I know,' said Jennifer.

'The verdict was accidental death,' continued Estelle.

'Go on, You obviously want to tell me something else.'

'Only because it might appeal to your morbid imagination and sense of romance.' Estelle examined her nails, her eyebrows raised mischievously.

'Go on, Estelle, tell me.'

Estelle grinned, leant forward in her rocking chair, and then leant back. 'No, I won't.'

'Go on, Estelle.' For a moment she was angered by Estelle's delight in her power.

'Promise it won't put you off him?' teased Estelle.

'Go on, Estelle,' said Jennifer, dreading what she was about to say.

Estelle examined her scarlet nails again.

'You really want to know?'

Jennifer swallowed. She knew what Estelle wanted to tell her, just as in the past, before Martin had bounced into her life like an overgrown puppy, she had known things before they happened.

'Tell me,' she said, and it seemed to her she was opening the creaking door of an old empty house and seeing the darkness.

'Well, if you insist then,' Estelle leant forward conspiratorially. 'Although the verdict was accidental death, everyone suspected she had committed suicide.'

'Suicide?' said Jennifer softly.

'Don't look so appalled. I thought that kind of thing appealed to you. Youthful death, and all that . . . poignant, tragic, the kind of thing you write about. Emily Brönte willing herself to die, Joan of Arc going to the stake, Mary Shelley . . . '

'Oh stop it, Estelle, please. Stop it,' said Jennifer, closing her eyes tight, to shut out the blackness.

'Don't be silly,' said Estelle.

'I'm not being silly,' said Jennifer, opening her eyes, which had tears in them.

Estelle gawped at her. 'Oh, Jennifer, I'm sorry.' She jumped up, leaving her chair rocking, and came to sit beside Jennifer. She put her arm around her. 'I didn't mean to tease you. It's just that . . . sometimes you do need teasing.' Estelle stroked Jennifer's hair. 'Dear old Jenny. You really are so sweet and sensitive.' Jennifer caught a hint of envy in Estelle's kind voice. 'Everyone said how beautiful you looked last week. I think suffering must improve your looks. And Duncan said you were much nicer than usual, more open and sympathetic. With Martin, well, sometimes you seemed so brisk and competent you unnerved people.'

At the dinner party last week Jennifer had thought it odd that other people could see her when she could no longer see herself. It seemed to her that she was no one now, just a bewildered consciousness floundering in a world she no longer had under any sort of control.

One of the other guests had spent the evening leering at his pretty girlfriend. He had a wife and a child, but nobody Jennifer knew had ever met them. They were cooped up in some house in the suburbs while he lived it up in London.

Another couple, Duncan and Alice, had an 'open marriage', which essentially meant that he had affairs and she did too, occasionally, just to pay him back. 'It's their way of keeping together,' Estelle had explained. It was all so puzzling to Jennifer. It seemed there were no general rules, only private ones.

They were all standing on shifting sand with no laws to cling to.

At least Richard, with his gaunt face and his intelligence, had seemed to have some kind of integrity.

She remembered how concerned he had looked as she told him she felt she was mourning for Martin. 'Honestly,' she had confided. 'Only it's even worse because I have to cope with his being alive and yet not being with me. I have to cope with the knowledge that he is living with another woman. And, even if he were to come back, he wouldn't be the same person. The Martin I loved, the funny, decent one, has gone forever. He's pompous and solemn and cold now. And sometimes I feel I've died too — part of me has, the part which was Martin. And I feel that I'm facing the day of judgement every day. I feel so guilty. My husband has made me feel so guilty.'

She stared at him earnestly. He had smiled and nodded. His eyes were a slaty grey-blue and she could see pain behind them. The other people in the room were chatting and flirting and laughing. She and this odd, tall man with the prematurely grey hair seemed set apart. 'I understand,' he had said. 'But it's not necessarily a bad thing to feel guilt. It's only through mental suffering that people change, you know.'

'But I don't want to change, I want to return.'

He shook his head. 'That's not the way to live.' He ran his fingers through his hair so that bits stood up on end. His hair was stiff, like bits of thin metal.

42

'Although I shouldn't be doling out advice,' he continued. 'I haven't managed my own life awfully well, as a matter of fact. I've made serious mistakes and been unable to tell anyone about them. But you, you seem very open. Perhaps too open. Or perhaps not.' He frowned and looked puzzled.

'You see, I don't want a new life, I want my old one back,' said Jennifer.

His attention drifted away from her.

'I find it very hard to talk to people,' he repeated.

Even now she could remember the ache in his grey eyes and the atmosphere of tension about him.

'Look,' said Estelle, her arm still round Jennifer. 'If you really are still upset about Martin...'

'Still? It's only been six weeks, you know,' snapped Jennifer, suddenly back with Estelle. 'What do you expect?'

'Why don't you try to get him back?'

'Don't even know where he is,' muttered Jennifer. 'He went on holiday with her. Anyway, I hate him.'

'Well then, I definitely think you should go out with Richard Stevenson if he phones. It would do you good.'

Estelle's eyes glittered inquisitively.

Jennifer said nothing.

Later that day, in the loneliness of her house, slightly drunk after lunch with Estelle, slightly weary, Jennifer phoned up her father and asked him if she could come and stay for a while.

After Sarah had left Edward, Edward and Jennifer had lived contented, intellectual lives together, discussing books, going for long walks, like brother and sister. She wanted to return to those safe days. Estelle was very sweet, other friends were kind, but they weren't enough. She needed to be with someone with whom she had shared the past.

'Well actually,' he said, 'I'm rather busy working on a book right now. In a week's time, well, that would be terrific. But right now, well, unless you very much want to come over ...'

'No, it doesn't matter at all,' said Jennifer. 'Not at all. Speak to you again soon. I must rush now. Bye.'

43

She put down the phone. How her father had changed. He used to be so unselfish. With Sarah around he had had a compassion he lacked now. The distress Sarah caused him, and his love for her, had kept his heart soft. But as the years without Sarah passed, he had grown curiously cold, concerned only with himself, and his books, and with not being hurt any more. People find different ways of killing themselves, thought Jennifer.

5

'Come in, my dear,' said Mrs Maugham the next day. 'My goodness! How splendid to see you.' She smothered Jennifer with a kiss and led her through the hall into the dimly lit drawing room of her ramshackle house.

Jennifer gasped.

A huge crow bridled from the mantelpiece: back arched, beak open in rage, wings outstretched, about to soar onto its prey. Beside it was a little grey squirrel, one paw curled round a pine cone, looking at her plaintively, as though asking to be saved from its imprisonment on an old bit of wood. Next to the squirrel snarled a nasty little stoat showing off its sharp little teeth, curling its back, flourishing its pale brown tail. All over the room were dead stuffed animals and birds stuck on bits of twigs, in glass domes, on wooden platforms covered in moss sprouting bits of dried grass. Under one glass dome a weasel ripped open a mouse; on the floor in front of the fireplace two cocks fought, resplendent in red and orange, wings back, faces vicious.

'The dead are always with us,' said Mrs Maugham, noting Jennifer's dismay, and chuckled. It was a deep, manly chuckle, at odds with the overpowering femininity of her appearance. 'Now come and sit down, my dear, don't stand there looking terrified. There's nothing to fear from our poor dead fellow creatures. It's the living you have to watch out for.'

Jennifer smiled wanly and sank down into the cabbage-rose chintz sofa. Oh God, she thought, how ridiculous I am. Even a stuffed animal can frighten me now. Where is the poise I used to think I had? Where is the confidence which allowed me only a few

45

weeks ago to stand up in front of a classroom of high-spirited schoolgirls and make them pay attention? Here I am, a jittery wreck of a person jumping at sounds, at objects, my head crowded with shadows and demons.

'Now, my dear,' said Mrs Maugham. 'What will you have to drink?'

How solid Mrs Maugham looked, standing by an array of bottles, which as far as Jennifer could see all contained sherry. She stood with her legs slightly apart like a miniature colossus. Bulky legs, mammoth hips, cushiony breasts which tugged at the little pearl buttons of her flowery dress. And her face was solid too, and reassuring, as she looked down at Jennifer.

'Sherry, please,' said Jennifer. 'By the way I'm ... I'm awfully sorry I rushed off yesterday. I was ... I was late for an appointment.'

Mrs Maugham smiled magnanimously, and poured the liquid-gold sherry into two crystal glasses.

'I was glad to see you had been to our dear little church.'

Mrs Maugham's eyes were the same colour as the bright blue wings of the hummingbird in a glass case on the coffee table. The hummingbird was not stiff and mournful like the rabbit's head on the wall, the bison's head fixed between two gloomy landscapes, the huge spider pinned like a butterfly in a glass-fronted box beneath the rabbit. The bird was vibrant, its throat decked in iridescent turquoise and its delicate wings seeming to flutter as its long beak plunged into a pink paper hibiscus, tail flaring out into a fan as it hovered, expressing delight in flight and in the nectar it was sucking up into its tiny body. Its wings sparkled like the Mediterranean with the sun on it: blue and exotic and not quite real, too magical to be real, too like a dream of the sea, something far away, out of reach, something Jennifer wanted to reach simply because it was so far away from human trouble.

'There we are,' said Mrs Maugham, placing a glass into Jennifer's long white hand, as though it were an elixir to cure all her ills. 'Now let me sit beside you and you must tell me your problems. That's what I'm here for, you know, to listen. And perhaps I can help you a little.'

Mrs Maugham's body weighed down the sofa and all at once Jennifer wanted to giggle at the absurdity of it all. She took a sip of the sherry, which was cloyingly sweet.

'There now, that's better, isn't it, my dear?' said Mrs Maugham in a honeyed voice.

'Oh yes,' gulped Jennifer, still struggling with her desire to laugh.

Mrs Maugham took Jennifer's hand in hers and Jennifer felt the electricity of affection in her touch. She no longer wanted to laugh. She wanted to tell the medium everything.

She began to tell her that Martin had left her, and why, and how lost she was without him. And all the while as she talked Mrs Maugham nodded and looked sympathetic and made vague comforting noises, 'oh dear' and 'how terrible' and 'how painful that must have been'.

'The awful thing is, Mrs Maugham, I go over and over it all in my mind. It's as though the past had become, well, a novel with plot and characters and a moral message. I worked all the time. I was selfish.'

'My goodness! When women work hard and achieve a great deal they are selfish. Men in similar circumstances are called great or brilliant or dedicated. Heavens! Don't be so unfair on yourself.'

Jennifer sighed. 'I suppose you're right.' She regarded Mrs Maugham earnestly. 'It's just that I wish the pain would stop.'

Mrs Maugham nodded, encouraging her to go on. Jennifer screwed up her face, trying to find the words to explain.

'But it's so hard to achieve a balance. I want both, you see. I want love and marriage and I want my dreams. That's the problem. I have always wanted everything. I've tried to fill my arms with so much that I've dropped the lot.'

'Dear me,' Mrs Maugham wiped her forehead with a white lace handkerchief. Some of her thick yellowy foundation came off on the lace. 'How well you put it. Even when I was married such problems occurred.'

'Are you ... divorced?'

'Divorced! Oh no, my dear. He passed over many years ago,

just three years after our marriage! I was only twenty-one. It's for his sake I keep these stuffed animals. He had an interest in taxidermy, the poor thing. It was about his only interest, apart from trying to dominate me, which of course I couldn't allow. When he passed over I changed my name back to my maiden one, Maugham.'

'I am sorry ... I mean about his death ... I mean his passing away.'

Mrs Maugham's expression glazed over. 'He left me a great deal of money,' she said. 'Which has been very useful. But of course I should really have liked a child.' Her hard blue eyes warmed up again. 'I feel I would have made a good mother. I might have had a daughter of your age, my dear.'

Jennifer thought of her own tough, flamboyant mother, who had spent her life playing the role of Joan Collins in a sexy movie. As a child Jennifer had longed for a comfy creature who pottered about in the kitchen like other children's mothers, although of course Sarah had had a few major advantages over them: she didn't nag, she was never petty, she lived her life with enthusiasm.

On the coffee table, beside the hummingbird, there was an outsize box of chocolates with a photograph of a puppy on the lid. Being with Mrs Maugham was like being a child, protected, humoured, cherished.

'Dear Jennifer. I can't bear to see you looking so sad,' said Mrs Maugham, moving even closer. Her fragrance of powder and cheap scent recalled Jennifer's old ballet mistress, who had also been an engulfing figure. She had terrified Jennifer because of the long dark hairs growing out from a mole on her over-powdered cheek.

Jennifer took her hand away. She didn't notice Mrs Maugham frown as she did so. Jennifer's gaze had roamed towards the grey, dusty windows and the overgrown garden beyond. She wondered why Mrs Maugham had let it grow so wild. The garden seemed far away, veiled in grey, like an early morning scene before the sun comes up and dries away the blurred damp air of the night.

A rosewood desk rested in front of the windows. Its spindly legs were too delicate for this room with its monstrous animals and heavy velvet curtains. It belonged to somewhere with a piano and gaiety, with windows opening onto the sweep of a green lawn. Perhaps, thought Jennifer, I shouldn't have come here, perhaps I should after all have gone to some psychiatrist in a nice modern office.

'Now Jennifer,' said Mrs Maugham briskly. 'We must make an effort. We must be positive, my dear. Let us examine your situation. Heavens! I can't bear to see anyone sad.'

Jennifer's face nudged into a smile. How skilfully Mrs Maugham sensed her moods.

'My dear. I feel that your husband is someone who won't accept guilt. If he breaks a glass, it's your fault, isn't it?'

'That's right,' said Jennifer eagerly.

'Well, heavens! my dear. It's perfectly clear that your husband did exactly as he pleased and now blames you for his leaving you. You fitted in with him, not the other way round.'

'Oh yes. Yes, perhaps that could be it...' said Jennifer, the load of her guilt lightening.

'Personally I have never felt guilt,' said Mrs Maugham. She looked down at her stubby nails which were painted dark pink like the walls — or what could be seen of the walls between the stuffed animals and the paintings with their shining surfaces and glittering frames.

Mrs Maugham asked Jennifer question after question and as Jennifer talked she felt closer and closer to her, as though she were an old and dear relation.

Jennifer told her about the blackness which surrounded her on all sides and made life seem unbearably short and hopeless. She told her she had considered suicide. She swore that she never wanted to marry again. 'It's no wonder the figures are so high for second divorces. If I were to marry again I'd see how small problems could become big ones and give up before they even became big.'

'That's not the way to think, my dear,' said Mrs Maugham with

a curious grimace. She put her feet up on an embroidered stool —
she could almost have been enjoying herself.

'But Mrs Maugham,' continued Jennifer, 'what is the point of
having faith in a future when it's impossible to count on anything,
when people change, deaths occur, when there is nobody to trust
and nothing to trust in?'

'You can trust me, my dear,' said Mrs Maugham velvetly,
stretching out for a chocolate. She examined it, like a spider sizing
up a fly, before popping it into her mouth. Then she licked her fat
stubby fingers.

Jennifer told Mrs Maugham that all she wanted to do was to
slide back in time and put her arms round Martin on a night a year
ago when he wished out loud that they could return to the time
before they married, when they lived together in a rented flat. She
told Mrs Maugham how he had stood at the door and murmured,
'We were happier then, we made an effort,' and how she had
looked briefly round from her desk and then continued to type her
life of Emily Brönte. In her imagination she turned round from her
desk and smiled radiantly. Then she stood up and came towards
Martin with that same loving smile on her face. She put her arms
around him and kissed him.

'Let's do that, darling,' she said.

Now she stretched out her arms to meet him through the past
but he no longer existed.

'I love him so much, you see.'

Mrs Maugham plumped up the cushion behind her.

'Perhaps I should see a psychiatrist, Mrs Maugham.'

Mrs Maugham took a sip of sherry. 'That would be an unnecessary expense, my dear, especially as I should be happy to help
you through this. All you have to do is to stop stretching out to the
past and accept what has happened. In time you will calm down.
Everyone has these periods in their lives. But the spirits are here to
help us get over these things, the spirits who are here now, with us
today, listening and watching and guiding us. You see, my dear,
we walk into the centre, into the spotlight, for a few years. And
then we die and move back to the wings and observe the other

people act out their lives. The spirits wait. They stand around us, prompting us, protecting us.'

Jennifer's eyes were drawn again to the hummingbird, and she envied its freedom from the problems of having life.

'Or, of course,' continued Mrs Maugham steadily, 'or, of course, there is another way. Some people choose to step out from under the bright lights earlier than they have to when life becomes impossible to bear and they are tired of the pointless gesturing and shouting. They choose to join the listeners in the shadows, away from the glare and the pain. But you are too young, too pretty, too talented, to choose that path. You have too much to offer the world.' Jennifer could smell the chocolate on Mrs Maugham's breath. The older woman's words recalled disturbingly how her Aunt Stella had spoken of 'pointless gesturing and shouting' just a few days before her death.

'Have another chocolate,' proffered Mrs Maugham, breaking the curious silence created by her speech. She made herself more comfortable on the sofa. 'They're delicious ones. My favourites. A client gave me them. Aren't people kind? Nothing's too much trouble for some of my clients. Heavens! They pay me such compliments too. But really I'd be nothing without my helpers on the Other Side. Nothing at all. Now, my dear,' she patted Jennifer's knee, 'I can't give you a sitting, I'm afraid, because your mind is too tense. We mediums are like radios receiving thoughts and messages from somewhere outside our earthly understanding. Your tension would provide far too much interference.'

Something scratched at the door and Jennifer jumped.

Mrs Maugham laughed.

'Don't be nervous, my dear, it's just my little dog. I don't allow him in here because he barks at the other animals and tries to attack them. So stupid, such a stupid little dog.' She ran her nails over her stockings.

Jennifer suddenly could hardly breathe and wanted to get out of this airless room and away from the noise Mrs Maugham was making on her stockings.

'I think I'd better be going.' Jennifer glanced at her watch and stood up abruptly. 'You've been very kind. I've imposed on your kindness.'

'Not at all, not at all,' chattered Mrs Maugham as she heaved herself up. 'Come back and see me. Come on Tuesday, at about four. You can meet my little group. There's my brother Stephen, and my young helpers Lily and Mike. We relieve suffering. With the help of the spirits, of course.'

'Yes. Fine. I'd . . . certainly I'll come, if I have time.'

Jennifer opened the door and the Yorkshire terrier threw itself at its mistress, yapping with pleasure. It had a little pink bow around its neck. 'Dear little Yorky,' said Mrs Maugham, stooping to pat its head. 'So affectionate.' She took him roughly by the collar to prevent him entering the drawing room.

In the hall Mrs Maugham repeated her invitation for Jennifer to return on Tuesday.

Jennifer stared at the floor. The house smelt strange, like the church, and the tightness in her stomach warned her of what she wished not to know.

'Do come, Jennifer. I'll be there too,' said a voice from the stairs.

'My brother Stephen,' said Mrs Maugham sternly. 'I didn't know he was here. He's always turning up when he's not expected.'

The man came down the stairs in his slippers by the wall coated in dingy brown paint, by the pictures in chipped frames, and his smile was thick and sensual, his eyes narrow in the folds of his face. Mrs Maugham switched on the hall light and the man cast a long dark shadow behind him. He had the spreading nose of a boxer and a waxy yellow skin. Even his white hair was tinged with yellow, and was greasy. She could see hairs growing out of his nose and there was a white stubble over his chin. His grey suit looked like one of Hitchcock's cast-offs; it hung loosely round the man's shoulders and his legs.

'Nice to meet you, my dear,' said a low voice with a hint of cockney. 'I've heard so much about you.'

'Have you really?' muttered Jennifer. 'How nice. I'd better be off now.' She grappled with the doorknob. The silence of those watching eyes was ringing in her ears. She couldn't open the door.

'Let me, my dear,' said Stephen Maugham, approaching.

'Go away, Stephen,' snapped Mrs Maugham, and released the catch.

Jennifer bolted out in the deserted August street and waved goodbye without turning round.

Later that day she sat at the kitchen table. I need something to calm my nerves, she thought morosely. Tonic wine perhaps. Soon I'll be resorting to tonic wine.

The fridge was humming, the clock was ticking and all the objects in the room were gaining a new definition. The pepper grinder stood in front of her like an oversize chess piece. A bottle of Perrier towered to the left; 'Naturally sparkling'. And by it was a corkscrew and a wine glass with a narrow stem. The objects were all stiff and formal, as though they had quarrelled and were now isolated in their separate griefs.

She remembered Stephen Maugham and shivered. How cold the house was nowadays. She was sure it was not usually so cold during the summer months.

The television sat on the sideboard by the sink, staring at her with its one big, square eye. On the wall, the white phone clung like a limpet.

The phone rang and Jennifer started. Martin: could it be Martin?

She watched it for a few moments then went over to it, her heart made of lead because she knew it wasn't Martin. She knew it would be Richard. The door was opening again into that house full of shadows.

'Hello. Is that ... is that Jennifer?'

'Yes.'

'It's Richard here. Richard Stevenson. We met at Estelle's party. Do you remember?'

'Yes, I remember.'

'How are you? You sound very solemn.'

'I'm fine,' she said in a distant voice which did not seem to belong to her.

'Good. Well, I was wondering. Is there any chance, well,

53

would you like to ... do you like films?'

'Yes, of course I like films. Some films.'

'Well, I very much want to see *Russian Revolution*. Have you seen it? Are you free tomorrow evening? It starts at eight.'

She said nothing.

'Are you there? Jennifer?'

'Yes,' she said. 'I'm here.'

'Eight at the Leicester Square Odeon. Please. I very much want to talk to you. There's something important I need to tell you.'

After she had agreed to meet him and he had rung off she went round the house closing all the curtains.

In bed that night she tried to read a copy of *Cosmopolitan* but its cheeriness depressed her.

She began a letter to its problem page on the back of a used envelope. The letter eventually covered the backs of four envelopes and one circular from the *Reader's Digest*.

She wrote:

Why is it that most people seem happy — your magazine, the television, the streets, restaurants, are all full of smiling faces — and yet I can hardly stand the thought of getting through tomorrow? Each day is like some huge mountain I have to climb. And I don't have the equipment any more. I've spent my life determinedly trying to turn myself into the person I want to be, and I succeeded, I suppose. Your magazine would probably admire me.

But my husband has left me and suddenly nothing means anything and I feel as though there's a ball and chain attached to my heart and I want this desperate unhappiness to stop. If there was some heroin near to hand I'd inject myself with it because I want oblivion. There isn't anything I wouldn't do to make this misery cease, this deadening of the spirit, this horror of the future. What can I do? It really is like a physical torture. I cry sometimes, and that helps, but more often I allow it to build and up inside me until the pain is so heavy I can't move or think.

Everywhere there are exits out of life — in the river, in the knife drawer, in front of every passing car. Or else one could choose a slower death: drugs, cigarettes, drink. Do you think it is wrong to take one's life even when it becomes a torment? You see I have lost myself. All my frontiers, all of what I thought was real, have been blurred by my dear husband's exodus. I am standing on sinking sand in a land of mists. It seems to me that suicide would be a way of re-finding myself, of creating my own destiny once again, as my heroines all controlled their destinies. Surely you can understand that? Isn't that brave? Isn't that the kind of courage your magazine admires?

My guess is that most car crashes are suicides and most old ladies run over by lorries allow themselves to be so on purpose. The climbing accident isn't an accident. Drowning isn't an accident. Aeroplane pilots want to die when they crash their planes. And when nuclear war ravages our world, that won't be an accident either.

We all have to leave this world sooner or later and why not when we want to? Why not control one's destiny in this way as well as all the others?

I'd like to know, please, why it's so wrong and what other ways there are to escape from my present despair. Time, you'll probably say, time will help you to escape but the thing is I have to live through that time, not you. You don't have to suffer my seconds, my minutes, my hours of desolation. If only one could be operated on, and have the misery cut out. Perhaps in time that will happen: a part of the heart or a part of the brain cut out for ever, a kind of suicide.

Please write to me and suggest the best way out of my intolerable state of mind.

Yours faithfully,
Jennifer Hamilton

She read the letter through and then tore up the envelopes one by one.

6

That night she couldn't sleep and she thought back on Martin's last visit to the house as she lay tossing and turning, the blackness of night pressing against the windows.

Once, Martin's beaming face had acted on her like a tranquiliser, calming each molecule, each atom, of her body. But that day, a few weeks ago, when he had returned to collect more of his things, his features had been disordered by cheeks slightly flushed from drink. The two hectic blobs had sat on his cheeks and his voice was slurred. He was no longer an affectionate puppy of a man, full of love; he was just a rather drunken person. She recalled with self-loathing how she had berated him for entering without ringing the bell.

'I did ring. And if you hadn't had a Walt Disney film on the television at top volume you might have heard me,' Martin had said with a grin.

'Rubbish!' she had replied, turning down the volume slightly as he edged to the door. 'Isn't it odd,' she continued, 'that we spent eight years enjoying each other's company and now suddenly you can hardly stand being with me for more than two minutes?' There were tears brimming up in her eyes.

'Don't cry,' he said, frowning. 'Please, baby.'

'I can't help it.'

He had taken her shoulders and kissed her gently on the forehead. 'I think I'd better get my things and go.'

'Go? You want to go? You see your wife like this and all you think of is going. I don't understand you, Martin. I've never understood you. You seem so sweet and yet you can be so horrid.'

'Look,' he said painfully. 'Let's lunch soon and discuss everything sensibly. We're not getting anywhere like this, especially when we have to shout to be heard over that programme about bears.'

She shook his hands from her shoulders, stalked over and switched off the bears. Martin hovered by the door of the kitchen. She didn't offer him a drink because that would have made him seem even more of a guest.

'I'd better go,' he said. 'I don't think I'm all that popular.' He smiled. His hair and beard were cut short. It made him look rather ordinary and accentuated his hooked nose. For a moment she hated Martin profoundly. He wore a new pale green cotton jacket and was moving restlessly from foot to foot, longing to remove himself from her presence. How dare that woman make him cut his lovely wild hair and trim his beard? 'I'd better collect my records and go.'

'There aren't any of your records here, Martin.'

He sighed. 'Jenny, let's not go through all this. You know this is what always happens to divorcing couples. They squabble over possessions. I can't bear this.'

'No. I don't think we should argue. If you just leave me with my records — which incidentally are all those upstairs — we won't quarrel at all.'

Jennifer had wanted a quarrel. She wanted scenes and recriminations. She resented the calm way Martin had taken their break-up. In the past she had admired his habit of not showing his emotions. Now she loathed it and even wondered if he had any to show. She wanted to see him upset. They were dealing with eight years of their lives and he was shrugging it off like a teenage date.

'Okay, if you want all the records, keep them,' he said. 'I can always get new ones.'

She longed to bellow something at Martin. She would have liked to have become hysterical. At least a loud scene would cause Martin some pain too, at least she wouldn't have to bear everything herself. She understood why people commit murder: to concentrate all their pain on someone else. But of course she would win nothing by making a scene. He'd just be calm and disapproving. She swallowed and moved closer to him. 'Martin, how can it all go, all that love, just like that?'

'I'll always be fond of you, Jenny,' he said, and she noticed the lines of his forehead which had been covered by his hair. He was getting older, and at the thought her heart jolted with love for him. She could not bear the idea of Martin growing old and dying without her. 'I wish this hadn't happened. I wish we'd made it work,' he said.

'I suppose it's like when one's depressed — all of life seems always to have been depressing; and when one's happy, one can't remember any other kind of feeling ...'

'Sorry?' he said.

'I mean that, because we're not getting on now and haven't been getting on for a little while, we both think our life together has always been like this. And it hasn't at all.'

'No. Of course not.' And Jennifer could see he was trying to think back, trying to remember the good times and not succeeding.

'Look, I really must be getting along,' he said. 'I'll just pop upstairs to pick up some clothes and then I'll be off.'

Grimly, she followed him up the stairs, past the pictures given to them for wedding presents, past the first-floor conservatory and its dying plants.

She stood at the door of the spare room and watched him choose which clothes to leave and which to take. He left a jumper she had always admired, and took one she hated.

'Are you happy?' she said in a strangled voice.

'Oh yes, quite,' he said, not looking at her. 'Most of the time.'

'I miss you.'

'It's no good, Jenny. We just have to face up to it,' he said, busily sorting his clothes.

After he had said goodbye, she had hurried to an upstairs window and watched him drive away. How precarious it all was, she had thought, how tenuous each person's hold on happiness. Once we have it we think it'll last for ever and yet it floats away so easily, sometimes when one looks away for just a moment.

7

It was strange to Jennifer how the world seemed beset by divorce
and crisis. Separating was like learning a new word in childhood:
suddenly one heard it everywhere.

Her friend Sheila down the road was considering leaving her
husband Tim for another man, Brian, one of her customers at the
toy shop in Covent Garden which she ran. Like Jenny and Martin,
Sheila and Tim had led separate, diverging lives. He frequently
worked late at home and had to spend nights away from home. She
had been out to lunch with Brian a few times and one evening had
had dinner with him when Tim was away for the night. She went
to bed with him because she was lonely, never expecting an affair
to develop, but it did. She fell in love with her Brian and he
fell in love with her and Sheila's peaceful life had been ripped
apart. She hadn't told Tim yet but knew she had to do so soon
because she simply couldn't bear the indecision. She called round
at Jennifer's house every few days and poured out her conflict.
Every few days Jennifer called round to Sheila and did the same.
They were very fair about the timing of these outpourings. Each of
them received about the same amount of talking time as they gave
listening time.

Jennifer had first met Sheila about a year previously. One
Sunday, Sheila had knocked on every door of the street asking if
anyone had found her black and white kitten, Tiptoes. She was in
tears. Jennifer had given her a cup of tea and a biscuit and had
liked the frail girl with the sad eyes. There had seemed something
bewildered about her as she sat on the sofa in tee shirt and jeans,
constantly stroking the pale hairs of her bare brown arms. She had

small hands, neatly painted with nail varnish. As a child, Jennifer had longed for pale gold hair and uniform features like those of Sheila, those of a princess, and had hated her own auburn hair and mobile face.

Sheila had the face of a lovely dumb creature and indeed had no grasp on anything outside herself: she never read newspapers, saw television programmes, had opinions about anything except people, food and clothes, which she wore with an élan which made her look French. Although she was articulate, witty and clever, she had never desired a career; she had only ever wanted to marry and have a family. Tim, however, had so far refused to let her have children because he said they couldn't afford them. Jennifer discovered most of all this on that first Sunday afternoon's talk, which ended only when Sheila's husband knocked on the door looking for her and saying that he'd found the cat locked in the hut at the end of the garden and it was having its dinner right now. She jumped up and clapped her hands like a child, and Jennifer had enjoyed her enthusiasm as she had enjoyed her anxiety, because in both moods she seemed more alive than most other people. After saying goodbye to Sheila and the stolid Tim, who reminded her a little of Martin, she had remembered George Eliot's words about Tom Tulliver in *Mill on the Floss*: 'A character at unity with itself — that performs what it intends, subdues every counteracting impulse, and has no visions beyond the distinctly possible — is strong by its very negations.' Often she wished she were more like Martin, and Tim, and Tom Tulliver, although she had always loved Maggie Tulliver more than any other character in a book.

On Sunday, Sheila's one day off, Jennifer called at her warm, sunny house, which was full of flowers and food and the stealthy movement of cats. They sat in Sheila's cork-tiled kitchen, whose French windows led out into the rambling garden. There were cats and kittens watching them from the floor, from the Welsh dresser, even from the top of the fridge.

Jennifer was surprised that Sheila had stuck with Tim as long as she had. He was always criticising her about something, in particular her job in the toy shop, which he said only encouraged her obsession with children.

Tim, Martin, Sheila and herself had had dinner together once. Tim had a slow, soporific voice and no strong views about anything. Martin and Tim had talked about politics, while Sheila had talked to Jennifer in a low voice about her customer by the name of Brian, which Jennifer had thought very rash indeed.

Tim agreed lamely with most of Martin's opinions and the discussion had just chuffed along like a very slow and old-fashioned train. And yet Sheila had appeared to rely on him. He was mild and respectable and had dry, wiry hair and a totally white face except for a few freckles dotted on his nose. He was extremely tall.

There were freesias on the table giving out a sweet smell of summer.

'I can't bear being parted from Brian, I love him so much. Yet I know if I run off with him I'll miss Tim for the rest of my life. If only I'd been good. I wish I'd been faithful. But it's so easy to be unfaithful and so difficult to be faithful.'

'I suppose so,' said Jennifer grimly, staring at the crack in the old pine table and wondering if this was what Martin had thought before leaving her.

'Oh, Jenny,' said Sheila, putting a glass of wine down in front of her. 'I'm so sorry. It's just ... What do you think I should do?'

Jennifer looked up. In white skirt and blouse, her skin slightly tanned, Sheila looked as though she should be lounging on some yacht being pampered and cherished, not torn apart by such indecision.

'I don't know. I really have no idea,' said Jenny.

'I can't choose between them, you see, and it's driving me mad. Love can be so different, can't it? I love them both in different ways and in some of the same ways. For instance, I couldn't imagine them both being in the same room together. They seem to be the same person. It's the conflict that's so terrible. I can't give up Brian. I just couldn't do it. And yet I can't go on lying to Tim. I really just do not know what to do.'

She sighed a touch histrionically, half of her clearly enjoying the romance of the situation, seeing herself as a romantic heroine. Sheila was so pretty that it surprised Jenny that she hadn't had an affair before. Most people seemed to, she thought crossly, regretting all the affairs she hadn't had, all the friends who had remained just friends, all the flirtations she'd never allowed to develop. What a mistake it had been to assume that Martin wasn't having any affairs, to think happily that his love for her precluded that possibility, that she was the centre of his life. She could have spent afternoons in bed with different men, with different lips, eyes, noses; she could have had sweet, warm, new tongues all over her body, moistening her nipples, pushing into her ears. She could have gone for romantic walks, had picnics with champagne, had rough hands running all over her. She had given up all this for nothing, for a lie, for a person who didn't exist; the faithful, virtuous Martin. And now she had no one to lie close to in bed, now the other pillow beside her was never creased. She scowled at Sheila.

'But would the love definitely continue, that's what I need to know,' mused Sheila. 'If only one could know that. If it did, it would be worth leaving Tim for.'

'I don't know, Sheila.'

'It's awful, Jenny. It's an awful mistake to have an affair. They cause nothing but pain.' She put her head to one side and smiled. 'But it is exciting. It does make one feel alive.'

A cat jumped on Sheila's lap and she stroked it again and again and again. It mewed in sensual delight and she kissed its soft tabby fur. 'My baby,' she whispered into its ear. 'My darling.'

Jennifer told Sheila she was going out that night with someone called Richard she'd met at Estelle's dinner party. Sheila smiled in vague interest and continued to rub her face against that of the mewing cat.

Oppressed by the brooding atmosphere of Sheila's house, Jennifer soon returned home. She was envious of that glow on Sheila's cheeks and the smell of freesias and cooking which pervaded her house. Jennifer's smelt of nothing but books. There were books in the lavatory, ceiling-high bookcases in the study and the sitting room, books on the kitchen shelves. Now Jennifer was fed up with books and her efforts to emulate the lives of glorious, ambitious women. For what had the admirable lives of heroines — of Joan of Arc, George Eliot, Emily Brönte — what had they done for her? She had studied them, written about them, and now her obsession with them had left her alone in an old house. She received fan mail for her books, usually from young girls of ten to thirteen. They too wanted to forge their own, unique lives. In her more defeated moments she felt like writing back to them and telling them not to bother, to take a course in domestic science instead.

Jennifer dressed to go out with Richard with great care and a good deal of nervousness. She applied her make-up according to the double-page spread in a woman's magazine she propped up in front of her. She wore a white silk bra, purple silk dress and high heels. She sprayed herself with scent. She wanted to be alive and feminine like Sheila.

Just before she left the house her father rang and asked her in a formal voice to dinner the following evening. 'Your mother will be there. We have been talking on the phone and have decided we should all meet. She has something to tell you.'

'Why, is something the matter?' she said.

'We can talk about it tomorrow.'

She moved from foot to foot. She remembered that day thirteen years ago when Sarah had left them. She remembered the despair in Edward's eyes, the determination in Sarah's as she struggled with her suitcase, refusing help.

'Why have you agreed to see Sarah again?'

'I just thought it would be nice, that's all,' he said un-convincingly.

'After all these years?'

'More sensible to ask me why I didn't want to see her before, I should think. Look, I don't want to talk about it on the phone. Why don't you come here at seven tomorrow?'

'All right,' she said.

'You sound odd. Are you okay?'

'Not really,' said Jennifer.

'Oh dear ... but ... look here ...'

'I'll see you both tomorrow,' said Jennifer, putting down the phone, pleased to hear his concern, her mind and emotions in a flurry of disquiet. She was still upset as she walked briskly through Soho to the Leicester Square cinema where she had arranged to meet Richard. She tried to ignore the sick feeling in the pit of her stomach, but couldn't. After all these years why were they all meeting again?

The last time Jennifer had seen her mother had been for tea at Fortnum and Mason's a week after Martin had left. Sarah had swept in fifteen minutes late, wearing her black raincoat with the fur collar. At once Jennifer had felt short and scruffy and without style. With her red hair and big smile, she could look like a mischievous urchin but could not manage to be a sophisticated woman of the world however hard she tried. A nonchalant scarf round the neck would always come undone, her clothes creased the instant she put them on, her stockings laddered, and buttons fell off her shirts as though stuck on with just a light glue.

'Darling,' her mother had said as she had tossed her coat on the chair by Jennifer. 'How are you?' She had kissed her on the forehead.

'Not too bad,' Jennifer had said miserably.

Sarah sat down fluently, long legs crossed, black linen suit uncreased, crêpe-de-chine turquoise shirt showing the freshness of something only just bought. Her black hair was twirled into a bun.

She regarded Jennifer sharply. 'You seem a little pasty-faced,' she said. 'You really must go to a health farm. I insist on paying.'

The waitress in her little white apron took the orders for tea and toast but no cakes. Jennifer longed for the day when she would be able to sit beside her mother and not feel clumsy.

'Now, darling,' said Sarah, lighting a cigarette. 'You must tell me how you're feeling. It's obviously been a terrible shock.'

'Well,' said Jennifer ... and didn't stop talking for a good ten minutes while Sarah nodded and made sympathetic noises.

When Jennifer took a break to eat her toast, Sarah informed her that she should now be at a health farm making herself beautiful if she wanted to persuade Martin back.

'I don't believe I can,' said Jennifer.

'In two or three months you'll be able to, if you really want to. Not that personally I think he's worth it. As you know, he's far too intellectually conceited for my tastes. He stifled you. But wait till he starts phoning for the odd chat. That'll be the sign that he's missing you. He'd be a fool not to. There isn't anyone else like you — serious, severe, intelligent, and, most important of all, pretty,' she said, placing her hand on Jennifer's knee. Jennifer took it away quickly.

'The sex always fades eventually. He'll go off her. And he'll come running back. Not that you should take him back. He was far too boring and cold for you.' Sarah had long eyelashes and knowing eyes. Her features had softened with age. Her sexuality was now mixed with a wisdom which made her more peaceful to be with than in her hectic past. There were lines on her face but her voice remained the same, a low, inviting, resonant murmur.

'I know I want to hurt the woman he left me for,' said Jennifer. 'But I suppose you're right, I don't know if I want him back. I want him as he was before that woman seduced him. But the past is irretrievable, isn't it?'

'I don't know, darling. Different people have different experiences. It's very hard to generalise.' There was an expression on her face of such sadness and longing that Jennifer realised that, after all this time, Sarah still missed Edward.

That day, even in the low light of Fortnum's, amid the warm carpets and silver trays, Sarah had a greyishness in her skin. Age was creeping into Sarah's spirited body in spite of herself. Jennifer had been surprised at how her mother's ageing had moved her.

She had accepted Sarah's offer at Fortnum's that teatime gratefully. She went to the health farm. There, she lay on the massage bed every morning, having all the tension removed from her neck, her shoulders, her back, by skilled hands. They even massaged her forehead while the draught from the window moved the pale yellow curtains which surrounded the bed. Meanwhile her hatred of Annabel, her memories, her strategies for getting Martin back, her fantasies of making him jealous, were going round and round in her head. It was curious, she thought, how difficult it was to think clearly and how very tiring thoughts could be. After ten minutes of thinking about what had happened she felt as physically wrecked as if she'd just climbed the Matterhorn. She was surprised the masseuses couldn't hear the creak of the wheel in her head, like a hamster at night. Her mind ran through jealous scene after scene, a video she couldn't switch off.

She imagined seeing Annabel and Martin together in the Turkish restaurant where Martin had first told her about his affair. Jennifer walked straight over and, as Martin's mouth hung open in horror, she poured their bottle of wine all over Annabel's smart silk suit.

In the next scene Jennifer was sitting in the same Turkish restaurant with Richard when Martin entered alone. She watched with great satisfaction as he turned white and left.

In another episode from her private soap opera Jennifer slapped Annabel hard over the face, in another she swore at her, in a third she pushed her into Highgate pond while Martin laughed.

Jennifer took long walks, swam up and down the pool, went to exercise classes, dance classes, practised yoga. By the end of the week she was half a stone slimmer but just as unhappy. The problem was, it seemed to her, that life was terrible and that only being in love or being stupid or being continually distracted could prevent one seeing that. It was ridiculous to put the depressed in psychiatric hospitals. It was those who weren't depressed who were mad. The way to keep out of the hospitals and the suicide lists was not to look down from the trapeze. The trick was to hem oneself in with a house, a family, a routine, and just keep looking forward to the next day, but never any further. Jennifer had looked down and knew there was a long, long way to fall.

That night, on her way to see Richard, the Soho streets were an uneasy mixture of night-time attractions — restaurants, night-clubs, porno shops — and the fresh light of early evening. Images of naked women with colossal breasts shoved themselves in front of Jennifer's eyes, while the leaves of Soho Square fluttered in the slight breeze. The men idling their way through the streets showed signs of corruption: a leering glance here, an unshaven face there, clothes which didn't quite fit. She hurried on, although no one could have mistaken Jennifer for anything but an upright young woman. She had the innocent, severe look of one of Miss Jean Brodie's young ladies as she tossed her head back proudly in unconscious recognition of their admiration.

The film Richard had suggested was a newly released study of the Russian revolution which went on for three and a half hours and contained numerous Hollywood stars. It was one of those films which people talked about at tedious length on television, at lunch, all the time, and which it was essential to see in order to alleviate the boredom of these discussions.

As she came close to the cinema, she felt the familiar churning in her stomach and she wondered how many times, bathed and with newly washed hair and best clothes, she had hurried across Leicester Square and on up Charing Cross Road to meet some disappointing young man at some cinema or theatre — all the time fearing that the hem of her skirt was down, or that there was a stain down the front of her trousers, or that she'd forgotten to powder her nose.

How ignominious to be back on this teenage road again, presenting oneself to a series of males in the hope that they would want to see her again. Even as a teenager she had longed to be back home with her books, although female pride had meant that she also wanted to notch up admirers. Damn it, she thought, damn Martin, damn Richard, damn everyone. What I need is a sex change.

'Hello,' said a voice behind her.

She swung round. The lanky, thin-shouldered figure of Richard loomed over her. He brushed back his grey hair from his forehead and peered at her.

'How are you?' he said.

'Fine, fine,' she muttered. He was wearing jeans and a tweed jacket and looked disconcertingly eccentric with his tall frame, grey hair and gaunt face. 'Gosh, it looks as though the film is popular,' she said, looking over at the queues outside.

He patted his pocket. 'I've got tickets,' he said, in an imitation of a self-important man looking after his girlfriend well.

'Terrific,' said Jennifer as the horror of not knowing what to say next seeped into her voice. He didn't help her out. He just stood there while she gabbled on about how much she wanted to see this film. He was leaning down slightly like an adult listening to a small child. When she had finished her speech about the film, he nodded. She chattered about another film she'd seen. He nodded again. He suggested that they go on into the cinema as the film was about to start.

'Of course,' she muttered, blushing. 'Sorry.'

They struggled through the pushing crowds to the stalls. 'You don't smoke, do you?' he asked after they had sat down in No Smoking seats.

'No,' she replied perkily, and babbled about the times she'd been tempted to smoke. Already Jennifer was beginning to feel weary. They sat in the darkness watching the ice-cream advertisements and the trailers, while Jennifer tried to work out what topics she would bring up for discussion over dinner.

She glanced at him anxiously. She wished she'd had a drink before coming out: it would have made her less jittery.

Once the film started she relaxed a little and the familiar whispering darkness soothed her.

Every now and again she looked at Richard as he sat staring ahead at the posturing, shouting stars. His slow breathing beside her aroused her a little, and when his knee touched hers for a moment and then drew away she was surprised by the frisson it sent through her body.

Even here, in the peace of the cinema, she could feel the pent-up tension in his limbs and in his head.

She found herself wondering how he made love, as a huge crowd

69

gathered in Red Square waving banners and shouting. Sex with Martin had always been controlled, delightful, a thoroughly pleasant way of spending a quarter of an hour. But with Martin she had never known the ecstasy that others spoke of, only the momentary release of orgasm. Perhaps Martin had found real ecstasy, earth-shattering passion, with his new bloody woman, thought Jennifer, and her desire left her, replaced by jealous rage.

At the end of the film, Richard shook his head crossly as though trying to rid his brain of something. He surged out of the cinema, head forward like a battering ram, and she hurried after him feeling ridiculously like a dachshund pulled along by some striding master.

'What rubbish,' he announced, as they hurtled through the cool evening air. 'Absolute rubbish. I don't know how they dare to put such rubbish on.'

She wished she were back in those comfortable seats watching those images and enjoying the silent companionship of Richard in the anonymity of the cinema.

She followed his long-limbed stride into a brightly lit Italian restaurant.

He immediately ordered a double gin and tonic, and she asked for a Campari and soda.

He studied the menu malevolently, as though it were somehow responsible for the film he had just seen. His tweed jacket was a little frayed at the sleeves.

She muttered about going to the Ladies, grabbed her handbag clumsily and wobbled off on her not-very-high heels, which suddenly seemed absurdly high when she considered that this fierce man was watching her.

She applied more make-up and more scent among the cold white tiles. The mirror was cracked and there was no soap. Her elfish face in the mirror was a little too glowing, a little too bright. It was odd that her unhappiness had made her better looking. All that had been firm, resolved, content in her face had gone, and it was replaced by a fluidity, a vulnerability, a new softness. She

70

practised a smile into the mirror. Usually her smiles were far too wide, like the grin of a Cheshire Cat.

She delivered him what she hoped was a delicate little smile as she made her way towards him through the narrow restaurant, which was really no more than a corridor with tables on each side.

'What would you like to eat?' he asked as she sat down. He looked very uncomfortable. Compared to him, she really felt quite at one with herself. Some people must spend their whole lives feeling out of place in the world, she thought, and felt sorry for them all. She peered at the menu, trying to forget the sadness she was experiencing. In the past she had never had to cope with these sudden onslaughts of compassion.

Jennifer had trouble deciphering the menu because it was written in loopy Italian stained with wine marks. Those items she could make out she either had no idea what they were or was quite sure she did not wish to eat them.

'What are you having?' she said in a false, jolly voice.

'Spaghetti alla carbonara followed by the veal Milanese, I think. Or maybe I'll have the minestrone.'

He pushed the menu away and scowled in the direction of a waiter. 'Wish they'd bring us our drinks.'

'I'll have the melon and the veal please.'

He leant to one side and gesticulated at the waiter, who ambled over with their drinks. They ordered their food and Richard knocked back his gin in a few seconds. He still looked tense.

'Well, this is nice,' she said chirpily. 'Have you been here before? I do like the pink tablecloths.' In fact, the room was cramped and hot with disagreeably harsh lighting.

'Really?' said Richard. 'I don't much. Do you mind if I take off my jacket?'

'Not at all,' she said, wondering what on earth they were going to talk about. There was one thing she was most definitely not going to bring up, and that was his presence at the spiritualist church. Anyway, it might not even have been him, she reminded herself.

71

The man on the table next to them, across the narrow corridor, had a huge red face and three tiers of fat at the back of his neck. His companion was a woman with a limp face who just listened as he talked, and watched as he ate and ate.

'Do you go to the cinema often?' she asked, attempting an expression of rapt interest.

'Not often. It always makes me cross,' he said, putting his elbows on the table in a mannered fashion. 'It's the triviality that annoys me.'

'I bet you don't own a television,' she said.

He narrowed his eyes, as though he thought she was teasing him, which she was.

'That's right, I don't,' he replied, as though that were obvious, as though no right-thinking person could possibly consider owning one.

'So what do you do in the evening when you don't go out?' My God, she thought to herself, he's quite right when he says he can't talk to people. Any moment now and we'll be eating in silence like that old couple by the door who haven't said a word to each other since they came in.

'I read,' he said.

The waiter poured him a little wine. He tasted it, pulled a face and then looked up at the waiter and nodded politely.

'What?' she said.

'Sorry?'

'What exactly do you like reading?' she said, and wondered what on earth people usually talked about.

'Eighteenth-century stuff mostly. Biographies, essays, some novels.'

He's shy, that's all it is, she told herself.

She nodded, trying to get him to go on without her having to interject some darn fool question. He drank his wine. She couldn't imagine why she had found him so attractive earlier; he was being surly and insufferably uncommunicative.

'Why the eighteenth?' she said.

'I like the sense of structure, and shared values.'

'Oh honestly,' said Jennifer, in sudden exasperation. 'What do you mean by that?'

He sat back a little. 'I should have liked to have lived in a time of certainty, that's all.'

She glared at him and heard herself say, 'And your wife, was she born out of her time too?'

He drew his chair in. His lips were thin in his long, El Greco face framed in grey. His eyes stabbed into her like knives, grey steel. She wished she hadn't mentioned his wife.

'She should have been an eighteenth-century aristocrat. What do you know of my wife?'

'Nothing. Estelle mentioned her, that's all.'

'Estelle is a busybody.'

'She's sweet.'

'Yes, she's sweet.'

The red-faced man at the table across the corridor was roaring with laughter at some joke, no doubt his own, while his companion wasn't even smiling. It was becoming excessively hot. How grave Richard was, like some stiff-lipped, repressed parson from a novel by Trollope.

The waiters dumped the next course in front of them.

Jennifer and Richard ate for a while in silence.

'Is your veal edible?' he asked.

'Oh yes, it's fine,' she said, moving a tough bit of meat to her mouth.

She smiled at him emptily, and then her smile froze.

He was watching her with intense curiosity.

'By the way, I've been wanting to ask you. Do you go to that spiritualist church very often?' he said.

She looked at the pale brown peas she had pushed to one side of the plate.

The hum from the other tables suddenly seemed a long way away.

'No,' she said. 'No. I don't.' She took a sip of her wine. 'I hoped you hadn't seen me.'

'I saw you the moment you came in.'

73

'I . . . I only heard the very beginning of what the medium said to you, something about some relation, then I left. It wouldn't have seemed right to eavesdrop,' she said, blushing.

'Jennifer, what I wanted to ask you is this: have you ever known anyone who lived in Hill Road?'

She was so hot she was sticking to her clothes. Why don't they have a fan, she thought. She poured herself some water.

'Hill Road in Notting Hill, just near the church,' he explained. He was leaning towards her.

A woman in high heels tripped as she went by their table and a few men turned and stared at the short skirt stretched tightly over her bottom.

'Ah yes,' said Jennifer, finishing her glass of wine. 'Of course. My aunt. My Aunt Stella lived there. She's dead now.' She smiled into the distance like an air hostess, vague, bland.

'At number thirty-eight?'

'I can't remember the number, I'm afraid. Awfully sorry.'

The waiter took away her plate although she hadn't quite finished.

'Gosh,' she said. 'The service is quick here.'

'Are you sure you don't remember? You don't remember the apple trees in the garden?'

She looked at him quizzically.

'Oh yes, there were apple trees. But then I suppose an awful lot of houses have apple trees. Are you going to have any pudding? Since Martin left me, I've been out so seldom I think I will have something sinful like an ice cream. I haven't wanted to go out, you know, but then I haven't wanted to stay in either because I hate being by myself. I always used to comfort myself by thinking that whatever happened in life, I would always have myself. And now I know that one can't even rely on that. Odd, isn't it?'

'At home I have a photograph of you. I found it on the floor when we first moved in and I kept it. At Estelle's, when I said I thought I recognised you, that was why. I kept it because the girl in the photograph is very pretty. More than pretty.'

Jennifer said nothing.

'And the woman who owned the house before us was called Stella Campbell. She died. She was your aunt, wasn't she? It was her picture of you?'

He was leaning forward insistently. She wanted to push him away and run to safety.

'How funny. You must be right.' She pushed away the menu. 'On second thoughts I won't have a pudding. Just a coffee. All my recent emotional stress has made me so tired. I want to sleep all the time.' She looked at her watch. 'I must get home soon and get some rest.'

'I think it might be important for you to listen to me.'

'It's just ... just that I'm tired,' she pleaded.

'You know Mrs Maugham, don't you?' he said.

Jennifer nodded.

'And are you aware of what she's like?'

'I like her,' said Jennifer. 'She's very understanding.'

'Listen to me ...' A waiter was hanging about wanting their order. Richard took no notice. 'You know that my wife died, do you? I imagine Estelle told you that.' The waiter wandered off.

Jennifer nodded. His voice was very grim. She liked his voice. It had a number of different tones to it. But she didn't want to hear what he was saying at all. She especially didn't want to hear anything against Mrs Maugham.

'Well,' he said, closing his eyes and then opening them as if from a painful dream. 'My wife was a very beautiful girl from a rich family. She cooked lunches for a board of directors in the City and that's all she did. The rest of her time she just did her nails, washed her hair and smoked dope. All she contributed to the house were mirrors. She was always buying mirrors. There were mirrors everywhere in the house. She liked to look at herself. Everything had always been so easy for her, and for generations of her family, that she never tried at all. She got into moods when she wouldn't speak to me for days. She kicked dogs and cats because she disliked them. At first I was impressed by the way she didn't care. She seemed to be above everything, and more beautiful day by day, more like a painting than a person. She had long red hair and a strange,

75

freckly face with eyes that changed minute by minute. And then her moodiness became violence. One day she smashed all the mirrors.'

Jennifer watched the red-faced man who was fumbling in the pocket of his vast trousers for his wallet.

'And do you know when this started? Can you guess?'

Jennifer shrugged.

'When she became involved with spiritualism. You see, your friend Mrs Maugham called round one day saying she wanted one last glimpse of her dear friend Stella's house.'

'Mrs Maugham is just an acquaintance of mine, not a particular friend,' said Jennifer. She looked at her watch again.

Richard leant further forward until he seemed to be overwhelming her, although she was positioned as far back as she could be.

'Listen to me,' he said softly. 'Mrs Maugham went upstairs and we heard her in the room which she claimed used to be your Aunt Stella's bedroom. Mrs Maugham was talking away to herself. You should have seen my wife's face when Mrs Maugham came down and said that she'd seen her old friend upstairs and that she — that is, your Aunt Stella — was terrifically happy in her life on the spiritual plane. My wife . . .' He lowered his voice still more to say her name. '. . . Cynthia, well, her face lit up. She wanted to know all about it. She went to the church . . .' He paused. He took a sip of wine as if it were a medicine giving him strength. '. . . she went to that church every Sunday and to private sittings at Mrs Maugham's once or twice a week; not that she talked to me about it. She cut herself right off from me. And she became very friendly with that horrible Stephen Maugham, who seems to hold some kind of perverse attraction for young women.'

'Could I have a cup of coffee?' said Jennifer.

Richard ordered two with a sharpness which made the waiter bow and hurry off.

'You know,' he continued, 'it's unusual for a young woman to be involved with spiritualism. Are you listening? Usually it's the older ones. She even went to what they call development circles. She decided she'd like to become a clairvoyant. They told her she

76

could. And she started to go crazier and crazier, or what I call crazy. She saw spirits . . . She saw your aunt, your Aunt Stella. She talked to her. And she often said she could feel her presence in the house like a cold wind over her skin.'

Jennifer finished her wine. She looked at her watch again. This was not at all what she had expected, what she wanted. He was talking and talking and not making sense. It was intolerable. She could experience his distress as if it were her own. She could see the face of Cynthia gazing into a mirror.

'She thought of nothing but the spirits . . . Honestly, Jennifer. It was terrifying. I didn't know what to do. And in the end, well, in the end she committed suicide. That's what I wanted to warn you about. That's why I wanted to see you so much . . . They are dangerous, Jennifer.'

Jennifer remained silent.

She stared at the fat man and limp woman. She did not want to think about the beautiful girl with the red hair. She had to get out at once. 'Please,' said Jennifer. 'I really do have to go. I'm — I'm expecting a phone call.'

'Please don't go,' he said. 'I'm sorry. I've distressed you. You're sheet white.'

'It's the heat,' she said wildly. She stood up. She fumbled in her bag for some money.

'Don't,' he said. 'Please stay.'

'I have to go now,' she said.

She hurried down the corridor. She saw Cynthia's face smiling coldly. She could hear the babble of the customers. Her heart was racing. She pushed the glass door and was out in the dark street. She took a deep breath of air. A couple of teenagers jostled against her.

'Jenny,' said his voice behind her. 'Let me give you a lift home.'

A taxi came down the road with its light showing. She hailed it. 'No, thank you. It's awfully kind of you. But no. I really must hurry home. It was a lovely evening. Thank you so much. I'm sorry to have to rush off.' She darted into the taxi without looking at him and slammed the door.

77

He banged on the window. 'I'll phone you,' he shouted, his face as pale and frightened as hers against the dark night.

She sank back into the leather seats, her heart still thumping, the girl still in her mind.

She didn't turn to look at him standing on the kerb, watching her taxi drive away from him.

8

The following evening, Jennifer arrived on time outside the dark blue door of her father's house. The light was on in the dining room at the front. It was painful to stand outside, the past tugging at her mind. She rang the bell.

Edward was laughing as he came to the door. She was the outsider. They were the couple. His blue eyes and gangling body stood above her. For a moment he seemed surprised to see her. And then remembered. How white his hair is, she thought, as she entered like a guest into the house where she had grown up. The paintwork was chipped and the carpet worn. Edward had lived here so many years that he didn't notice such things. The house had grown round him, grown old as he grew old, acquired paintings and books as he acquired memories. Edward had travelled a great deal over the years without Sarah. There was a rug from India, and another from Persia, in the hall. The dinner service in the dining room had been bought in Paris, and the glasses in Venice. Everywhere in the house there were paintings and etchings bought from street markets and shops all over the world.

It was in this house, thirteen years ago, that Jennifer had first met her mother's architect lover, Paul, who had broken up Sarah and Edward's marriage and made fifteen-year-old Jenny fall in love with him. Occasionally, Jennifer would receive a letter from Paul. It was strange to think he was now in his thirties. He'd been married twice, divorced twice, and had recently started his own business — designing and putting up conservatories — in California. Paul sounded as insecure now as he'd been before, when he'd beguiled both mother and daughter.

Jennifer followed Edward up the stairs and into the first-floor living room, where Sarah sat in the armchair looking frail in a black suit. She smiled weakly. She had a gin in one hand and a cigarette in another.

'Your mother isn't well,' said Edward. 'That's why we're meeting today.'

'I have a tumour, as a matter of fact. In the stomach,' said Sarah. 'It's very sudden.'

Jennifer stood stiffly, staring at her mother's ashen face and the shadows under the eyes. She was horribly changed from that day at Fortnum's. Jennifer rushed over and kissed her. Sarah drew back, embarrassed at the warmth and pity of Jennifer's embrace.

Edward busied himself finding Sarah ashtrays, pouring her drinks, asking her if everything was all right. She had arrived at five. Edward had therefore had a good three hours to talk but he still had more to say, and more to ask. He looked the same as ever, tall, kindly, shabby in paisley shirt and baggy grey trousers which matched his gentle eyes.

In a matter-of-fact tone, Sarah told Jennifer that she could be dead in a few weeks if the operation discovered the cancer had spread to the liver. Even if that were not the case, the operation might still not work. On the other hand, it might. She was being admitted to hospital the next day.

In spite of the unhealthiness of Sarah's face, her lines, her thinness, her air of weariness, Edward watched her face incessantly. Jennifer wondered if she'd still love Martin if he were to return in thirteen years' time.

As Jennifer sat in the darkened dining room, the candlelight illuminating Sarah's face, she once more felt out of things. She did not belong here as she did not belong with Martin. She could see Edward's distress as Sarah pushed most of her food to the side of her plate and sighed theatrically. The three of them had sat in that dining room so many times that the space between them was full of unresolved emotion.

How different Sarah was now from the vivid creature who had sat at this same dining table, in this same room, all those years ago.

Sarah looked at Edward with a gentleness which Jennifer had not seen in her before. When they moved upstairs for coffee, she had to drag herself up, as though the weight of her whole gaudy life were weighing on her thin shoulders.

She sat down with a sigh. 'I've lost two stone in the last month. I kept thinking I was imagining my ill health. I drank more to perk myself up and I knocked back masses of vitamin pills. I even started running. But the first time I tried I fainted after five minutes. It was infuriating, the way my body just would not keep up with my will.'

'You're tired, darling,' said Edward softly. 'Perhaps you should go back, don't you think, Jennifer?'

'Yes. Shall I call a taxi and drop you off at your hotel, mummy?'

'What about coffee?'

'Well, perhaps you could stay just another half an hour,' said Edward, his eyes still entranced by Sarah's presence.

When the taxi arrived, Jennifer and Sarah kissed Edward on the cheek. They left him alone on his doorstep, waving, as their taxi drew away in the rain.

'I'm too weak to talk,' murmured Sarah, as she slumped back in the leather seats.

Jennifer looked out of the window at the wet streets.

'Edward is as lovely as ever, isn't he?' said Sarah briskly.

'Oh yes,' Jennifer paused. 'He has missed you very badly.'

'I know. We should have seen each other before. We were both proud fools,' she said firmly.

'It's a pity, that,' Jennifer said.

Sarah suddenly crumpled. She became even smaller than the small figure she'd been all evening.

Covering her face with her hands she began to sob. She sobbed so hard that it seemed her insides might come out.

'Please don't cry, Sarah,' said Jennifer desperately. 'Please don't. Everything's going to be all right.' She put her arm round her mother. 'I feel sure everything will be all right.'

Sarah continued to sob violently until they reached the hotel where she was staying. Then she sniffed and blew her nose.

Redness had replaced her earlier pallor. She stepped out of the taxi with an air of dignity, then began to sway. Jennifer started to climb out too but Sarah stopped her. 'That's fine. Leave me, darling. I'll be okay.' She blew Jenny a kiss. Jennifer watched the fragile, suddenly old, figure walk up the shining steps into the golden light of the hotel.

Jennifer's house was deadly silent when she entered. It was so still that it seemed it could never have been full of movement and noise. She could not bear its deadness. The pictures they had chosen were on the wall, the curtains were hanging up, the house was like a body prepared for a funeral. It had no life left in it, only a pretence of life. She went through the kitchen, with its apricot walls, out into the blackness of the garden. It was still raining a little.

'Oh, Sarah,' she whispered.

The smell of honeysuckle reached her and reminded her of lost time, of all the moments missed, the things undone, the might-have-beens which would never happen now. You cannot return, she told herself, you cannot return to where you were before it all went wrong. You cannot deliver that smile, make love that night, go out to that dinner. You cannot adjust the past.

But that night she phoned Martin and asked if she could see him the following day.

9

Martin was late for their lunch. She sat at the table by the window and stared out at the people passing by. She felt very sad for them all — all the poor lonely creatures stuck in the solitary confinement of their skulls: the old man, his suede shoes dark at the tips from the rain, who shuffled along carrying two cans of beer; a girl standing alone at a bus stop in a headscarf; a young man gazing down at his feet as he walked.

They were the people who, at night, going home to their loneliness, passed by windows misted up with other people's pleasure. They saw this scene here, in the restaurant, and envied the collage of bright clothes and confident smiles. Grouped together in forgetfulness, the restaurant guests ate and drank and gossiped as if on a cruise which would last for ever. How easy that thin black-haired girl at the next table appeared to find living. She really seemed to have got the hang of it. She talked avidly, listened efficiently, laughed every now and again in such a carefree way that her partner (who had his back to Jennifer) must surely have adored her. Jennifer wondered if the black-haired girl had been born like that or whether she had struggled to achieve this command over her existence. What was unfair about life was not that some people were born rich and titled and others poor, or even that some were clever and some weren't; the real unfairness lay in people's varied capacities for happiness. If only she had been born with a sunny disposition, she thought gloomily, and remembered again the ache in the eyes of Richard when she had left him white and frightened in the night which was her night too.

'Jenny!' She looked up and her heart lurched. Martin was

coming towards her with that confidence she loved and needed so much. He was grinning and his hair was untidy and suddenly everything was all right again. He looked as chaotic as ever in his shetland tank-top and white shirt with the sleeves rolled up.

He regarded her warmly as they ordered their food. It was curious how normal everything seemed. He looked the same as ever and yet he wasn't the same. She couldn't understand how he could look like her Martin and not be her Martin. While they discussed the ideal distance between tables in a restaurant, she wanted to ask him *why*. She wanted to know why he had left her for that girl. She wanted to lean over and, in a low voice, ask just what it was about that girl which made her so special. Was it her bottom? Did she have terrific breasts? Was she — Jennifer would ask, with a polite smile — perhaps skilled at a particular sexual position?

'How's your flat?' she said into the next silence.

'Wonderful. It's a smashing place. Although I really must move my books in, too, soon. How's the house?'

'Fine. But too big for me.' She dug her spoon into the hard avocado.

'You're bearing up then?' he said, anxiously.

'Oh yes.'

Jennifer wiped a segment of prawn from her wide lips. 'By the way, my mother's going into hospital. To St Matthew's. She has a tumour. I'm visiting her tomorrow.'

A blank expression passed over his face. 'I'm sorry, I really am,' he muttered.

'I'm sure she'll pull through. Sarah is so resilient. Do you remember my telling you . . .'

They talked and talked and the only difference from the past, when they had been happy, was that, as they talked, Jennifer became more and more exhausted. It was as though she were floating on the surface of a sea, apparently buoyant, but in fact pulling against the force of a whirlpool trying to suck her down. Martin seemed as level and unemotional as ever. He is lucky, she thought. It is odd how little he seems to value his ability to be content and easygoing. It is really all that matters in a man's life and yet money, power, fame, were what interested everyone.

Martin poured another glass. 'How is your George Eliot book getting along?'

'Slowly.'

'Perhaps you should leave it and take a holiday. You do work too hard, you know. You get obsessed.'

'Maybe you're right,' replied Jennifer. 'By the way, is your girlfriend — Annabel — all right? All going well, is it?'

'Oh yes. Terrific.' He swirled his wine about in his glass. 'But the surprising thing is that, although she's so high-powered, she's very insecure about her work. Much more so than you.' He stared past Jennifer and looked a little bewildered.

'But apart from that everything's terrific,' said Martin brightly, as if the news would please Jennifer. 'We're thinking of buying a house. Annabel's father is putting up the deposit.'

Jennifer's grip tightened on her paper napkin.

She pushed away her food. Martin was always on the lookout for the main chance, she decided. He was a manipulator. 'By the way, are you in need of some more money?' said Martin, lowering his voice. 'I do know that the house is expensive to run. Annabel is very concerned that you should have more money if you want it.'

'How very kind of her,' said Jennifer.

'Oh, Jennifer, please don't become cross,' he said peevishly. 'There's really no point. I want you to be happy. You know we two weren't happy together. Things will be much better for us both now. Personally, I'm convinced of it.'

'Martin, you are twisting the past. It wasn't the way you see it now. It's bad enough that that girl of yours is trying to change our future. It's unforgiveable of her to try to change our past.'

'I don't understand what you're talking about.' He laughed. 'One great advantage of Annabel is that she doesn't read very much and doesn't ever indulge in psychological analysis. She wouldn't dream of trying to change our past. Do buck up, Jennifer. I know you're upset about your mother but you really must try to pull yourself together.'

For one heady moment, Jennifer thought she might let herself go. She wanted very badly to knock over the table. She would have liked to have thrown the remaining wine in her glass at Martin's self-satisfied expression. She wouldn't have cared about the gawping faces in the least. That upper-class girl with the pony tail, that fresh-faced young banker, that man with the pin-striped suit. They were all pretending. They were all acting out their roles. Choosing the wine, sipping the wine, passing the salt, passing pleasantries. It was all a grotesque charade. Their mouths opening and shutting. Their talk about their jobs or their forthcoming holidays. What utter nonsense it all was. What an idiotic pretence. It was raining outside. They were warm and cosy in here, all huddled together, pretending. How shocked they'd be if she started to scream. But wasn't that in fact the appropriate response to life, to the losing of loved ones, to the illnesses which crept up and killed, to the certainty of oblivion, the inevitability of grief?

Martin was laughing as he ordered himself apple pie and cream for pudding. He didn't seem to notice her fury. Jennifer glowered and shook her head at the waitress, who smiled at her sympathetically, as though she knew what Jennifer felt. But Jennifer managed to control herself. She managed to act the part of a tranquil, well-adjusted young woman. She said very little and just let Martin talk and laugh.

What Jennifer hoped was that one day Martin would realise that he had made a mistake. She hoped he would realise that he loved her after all. It could happen. After all, she never knew how much she loved and needed him until he left her. The prehistoric monsters of revenge, hate, pain, which had been hibernating under his rule, nowadays regularly came lumbering and crashing and shrieking through her brain.

She decided to pity Martin. He had been stupid to walk out on her. He would now spend his life wandering from woman to woman with no centre to hold him. Or she hoped he would.

'Do you always go everywhere together, you and Annabel?'

She remembered how she used to hate him when he came back

from a party. He used to have the smell of other people about him, of smoke and garlic.

'Always,' said Martin proudly. 'You see, I've come to understand that one has to work at a relationship. By the way, are you . . . seeing anyone?'

'Oh yes.'

'Who?'

'Someone called Richard Stevenson.'

'Marvellous news,' said Martin. 'Do you good.'

She caught the edge of a slight irritation in his voice and decided to make the most of it.

'I've only been out once so far,' she said breezily. 'But I'm thinking of seeing him again. Might as well enjoy my freedom, don't you think?'

Martin's lips tightened. He shrugged. 'Perhaps we should be off now.' He looked at his watch. 'I've some students to see.'

10

After lunch with Martin, Jennifer went for a walk in Holland Park. She sat huddled on the grass by the side of the path with her knees drawn up, head down, wanting to disappear. She wanted to melt into the grey tarmac or vanish into the grass like a chameleon. The trees, the children, the strutting cockerels, were all part of a strange, blurred scene which was happening to someone else. How dare Martin be so thoughtless, so cold, so priggish? She hated him. How could her mother be ill? She was scared. She wanted to die. She wanted to smash something. She lifted up her head from her knees and wanted to kick that yapping dog, hit that sweet-faced kid, throttle that stupid duck. She didn't care. She didn't care what people thought about her because she didn't seem to matter any more. She hardly knew who she was so how could she mind what people thought?

A grey squirrel scurried up and regarded her cutely. She was about to yell at it but stopped herself, and sighed. How much easier it would be to let go of one's identity completely and be able to yell at squirrels or shout at passers-by or tear at one's clothes.

She looked at her watch. It was four o'clock, the time she had said she might visit Mrs Maugham again. She pulled out a blade of grass and chewed at it. Over the other side of the path were bushes of hydrangeas — lavender blue, violet purple, heavy pink. Above her a few clouds scudded carelessly across the sky. Mrs Maugham had been very kind, Jennifer reminded herself, very comforting. But supposing Richard were right after all, supposing his warnings were not just the ramblings of a crazy, repressed mind. It was so hard for her to judge now that she was half crazy herself. At the thought of Richard and his grave intensity, a warmth stole over her body and she tilted her face to the sun and felt its rays. She saw again his unhappy face and the urgency of his eyes. But Mrs Maugham was pulling Jennifer to her and it wasn't long before Jennifer found herself rising to her feet, hurrying across dry grass and grey paths under trees laughing in the rustling breeze.

The cab pulled up in front of Mrs Maugham's house in Notting Hill. Her side of the street was in the shadows while the pavement on the other side glittered in the bright sunlight. How tawdry and uninviting the house was, with its chipped paint and drawn curtains. For a moment she wished she hadn't come here. She needed sunlight and laughter, not drawn curtains and shadows. And yet perhaps she belonged in the shadows, among the shades, maybe that was why she had come here. She certainly had never felt a part of that vivid, smiling world which other people seemed to inhabit. She had sat at dinner tables feeling the wrong size, the wrong shape, unable to link up. She was always watching, trying to see how to behave, trying to remember the kind of things people talked about. And always she would have preferred to be alone, in her room, the curtains closed, working through the night.

A stick-like young man stood in the doorway; his skin was as white as paper and as thin, almost translucent. She gasped.

The Yorkshire terrier rushed yapping at her and the man's boot kicked it away. It cringed back, by the stairs.

'Is Mrs Maugham in?' asked Jennifer, clutching her handbag to her.

'She is. She's expecting you,' said the young man, whose skinny body was ill matched with his face. All his features looked as though they'd been moulded by some malevolent sculptor. The nose, the chin, the forehead, all stood out far from his eyes, which were small and piggy.

She followed his hunched shoulders and narrow hips through the dark hall into the drawing room, where the first person she saw was Stephen Maugham with that thick smile crowding his waxy face.

'Hello, my dear,' he whispered.

All at once Mrs Maugham was beside her, with her arm around her, guiding her to the sofa. She offered Jennifer a cup of tea and introduced her to the slight girl perched beside Jennifer, her knees clamped together.

'This is Lily. She so much wanted to meet you, my dear.'

Lily smiled at her with bleak eyes, and the smile seemed to have been grafted onto that long, tragic face, the colour of chalk. She looked no older than a schoolgirl: flat chest, a pleated skirt, a white blouse, flat hands resting on her navy skirt. She sniffed. The snub nose was slightly red.

The only light in the room was a small gap in the drawn curtains. Jennifer felt as though she were locked in a museum after dark with waxworks which had come alive. Her glance darted from person to person, then rested for a moment on the black glossy crow on the mantelpiece, its wings spread out, as though about to swoop.

Mrs Maugham picked a chocolate for herself with a pincer movement of her fingers. Then she retreated to the armchair and sank into it like a balloon deflating.

'This is Mike,' said Mrs Maugham. The stick-boy was hovering by the sofa. 'He works in a hospital providing solace for the sick. Stephen, well, dear Stephen is a travelling salesman. He journeys all over the country spreading the word. Toys, he sells, because he loves children.'

All the while, as Mrs Maugham talked, Jennifer could feel Stephen Maugham's eyes on her. They were powerful eyes but without any warmth at all.

'As for Lily, dear Lily works in a chemist's shop. She meets very many people there, ill people, unhappy people. We all hate unhappiness, my dear. We want to eradicate unhappiness.'

Lily was staring straight in front of her. Her mousy hair was pulled tightly from her face in a ponytail secured with a green rubber band. She turned her puffy eyes on Jennifer and managed a tense little smile.

Jennifer smiled back at her with her lips, but not with her eyes. The girl looked down, embarrassed.

'What is it, my dear?' said Mrs Maugham to her.

'I'm sorry. It's just that . . . I like Jennifer . . . she has an aura. She's one of us, isn't she?' asked Lily.

'That's right, dear,' said Mrs Maugham sharply.

'She's worried about someone, isn't she?'

'Yes,' said Jennifer. 'Yes, I am. My mother.'

'She'll be all right,' said Lily gently. 'Don't worry.'

'Lily thinks she's bloody Joan of Arc,' said Stephen as he pulled back the curtains and the sun shot through onto the worn patterned carpet, lighting up the whole room and making its inhabitants blink. In the daylight, the pale girl, the emaciated boy, the tramp-like man, seemed even more like creatures who belonged without sun, down below the earth. Far more like ghosts than the stiff, formal, dead animals, even more like ghosts than the two fluffy baby owls huddled together in the hollow of a log by the door, white and strange with the big eyes of night.

Lily looked at Stephen listlessly. 'He knows nothing,' she said.

'I know about women.'

'He's been married three times,' said Lily flatly.

'My mother,' said Jennifer. 'I just wondered how you . . .'

Lily turned again to Jennifer. She tucked her handkerchief up her sleeve and sniffed.

'I promise you, Jennifer. Your mother will live. Sometimes God sends us despair to awaken new life. He sends suffering to renew us. Our lives have a pattern although we cannot see it. It is a pattern of life and death, destruction and renewal. Some have to die, before they can be renewed; others, like you, have a choice.'

Jennifer noticed that the hummingbird seemed almost to be moving as it fluttered in perpetual flight. She could not quite understand its fascination for her, except that it looked alive when it was dead and that in its perfection it held out some hope that things were not as they seemed, that the ethereal, the spirit, the soul, could shine in the darkness as this creature shone in the half-light of this room of shades.

Mrs Maugham, Stephen and Mike were all glaring at Lily.

In a weary motion, like an old woman, Lily stood up. 'I think I'd better go,' she said. She was short as well as slight, her limbs brittle, like twigs. She was blinking at the hummingbird as though she had only just noticed it.

'I'm very tired,' said Lily. 'Very tired indeed. It's my cold.' She blew her nose.

'And you and Mike, you'd better go too,' said Mrs Maugham to Stephen.

'I was going anyway,' said Stephen truculently, swaggering over to Lily. 'I think I'd better take Lily off to her shop. The poor girl is a little over-wrought.' He took Lily's hand. She didn't resist, just gazed blankly in front of her.

'Goodbye, Jennifer,' said Stephen. 'We'll see each other again.'

He lumbered out. The little girl beside him contrasted with his ungainly form.

'That girl is quite remarkable. But a little presumptuous,' said Mrs Maugham.

Jennifer went to the window and stared out at the tangled garden. She watched a bee fly from velvet foxglove to gaudy hollyhock in the warm summer air. She didn't know whether she trusted in Lily's pronouncements or not.

'Suffering and conflict often bring out unusual powers which would be buried in a person leading an ordinary, comfortable life,' said Mrs Maugham.

Jennifer ran her fingers over the dust of the window. 'Do *you* think my mother will be okay?' she asked.

'If Lily says so, yes. She has a great gift of clairvoyance.'

Jennifer experienced relief and a returning affection for Mrs Maugham.

'Lily's a sweet girl but her parents never stop arguing and that's left its mark. It's made her escape into her world of voices and spirits. She really is remarkable and has learnt mediumship very quickly.'

'And how did *you* come to learn it, Mrs Maugham?' said Jennifer warmly as she sat down on the sofa facing Mrs Maugham.

Mrs Maugham came to sit by Jennifer. She was watching Jennifer closely as Jennifer took a chocolate, a walnut cluster, from the welcoming box beside her. 'Never mind me. Poor

Jennifer,' she murmured. 'You are in a state, aren't you?'

Mrs Maugham put her arm around her. For a moment it seemed that she and Mrs Maugham were the same person. Perhaps, she thought, this is Mrs Maugham's gift, this is what Cynthia gained from her, this relief from the loneliness of being locked in with oneself for a lifetime. No wonder Stella had adored Mrs Maugham. She was undoubtedly a good woman.

On the wall the bison's head looked down like a fairytale beast, so very sad, and Jennifer's heart went out from him to all the poor beasts, to the people in sadness, as well as to those who were hunted and suffering and dying.

'Mrs Maugham. Can I ask you something?'

'Of course.'

'Richard Stevenson. Do you know Richard Stevenson?'

Mrs Maugham stiffened.

'Of course,' she said coolly. 'Of course I know him. A very sad case.'

'What do you mean?'

'Suffering ennobles some people, others it turns sour. His dear wife's accident has made him paranoid, quite paranoid. Do you know him well?'

'I've been out with him.'

Mrs Maugham stretched out for a chocolate and bit it in two. She ate one half. Mrs Maugham wore orange lipstick which spilt off the edge of her mouth and marked one of her teeth.

'Does he know that you know us?'

'Yes. Yes, he does.'

Mrs Maugham put the other half of her strawberry cream into her mouth.

'He'll try to turn you against us, mark my words. He's knotted up inside, poor thing. Have nothing to do with him.'

The sun had gone in, and the room was dark again. Jennifer said she really must go, but Mrs Maugham insisted she stay a little longer. As she talked about her fears for her mother, Jennifer's heart became more and more leaden, although of course Mrs Maugham was sweetness itself.

11

When Jennifer finally left Mrs Maugham she was already late for her appointment to see her mother. At a stall outside the hospital she bought a bunch of pink roses.

When she entered her mother's private room she gasped. Sarah was sitting up in bed. She greeted Jennifer and the low sexy voice was the same as ever. Jennifer reminded herself of Lily's words.

'Sarah!' she exclaimed. 'You look ... you look fine.'

Sarah wore a salmon-pink satin nightdress. For once, her dress sense had failed her. The pink emphasised her pallor. 'I was about to put my make-up on. I wasn't expecting visitors yet. I'm sorry, Jenny. I know I look awful...'

Jennifer came to sit by Sarah on the chair beside her bed. She was clutching the bunch of roses. It was as though Martin's desertion had put a spell upon the whole world, changing it from something stable to something horrifyingly unpredictable. She saw death everywhere: in her mother's skin, taut over her cheekbones, in the corridors of the hospital, in the eyes of Stephen Maugham.

'Some days I look better than others, Jenny. Don't worry.'

'I'm not. I'm sure everything's going to go fine,' she said lamely.

'Really? Well, let us hope for the best,' said Sarah.

She took the flowers from Jennifer — who had completely forgotten them — and with a tender smile smelt them. The self-consciously brave voice and the smelling of the roses reminded Jenny of the actress in Sarah, the old Sarah who always did everything for effect. She was no doubt imagining Jennifer weeping over the memory of her mother's courage long after her death. It reminded Jennifer of the strength of her mother's personality, that she would pull through if there were any possible way she could do so.

'When is the operation?'

'In two days. Thursday. I'm supposed to be resting today and tomorrow to help build up my strength a little, and so they can do all the necessary tests. Do you mind if I put on some make-up? I'm afraid that Edward might turn up any moment. Could you hold the mirror?'

Jennifer held the hand mirror for Sarah while, with great care, she applied her foundation, her blusher, her highlighter, her thick mascara. She rearranged her hair, pulling down one or two tendrils and securing her black bun more firmly.

That's a bit better,' she said, pursing her lips coquettishly into the mirror. 'Edward's been so kind and I really don't think I should frighten him out of his wits.'

She powdered her nose. 'There, thank you so much,' she said graciously, as Jennifer put down the mirror.

'My nurse here says a tumour in the stomach is terribly serious. Gloomy little chap he is. But I don't believe in taking any notice of those kinds of people. I personally think you can fight your way out of most things, cancer included, with a little bit of luck, and I have always had more than my fair share of luck.'

'Oh, I'm sure of it. You'll pull through.'

'Do you really think so, Jenny?' said Sarah, more softly.

'Of course.'

'Everyone's so kind. I really mustn't be feeble.'

The room had bouquets of flowers on the windowsill, on the table, everywhere, covering up the drabness of the yellowy walls.

'I'm not encouraging visitors because I know I don't look my best, and to be honest I get worn out so easily at the moment. But I've received countless cards and, as you see, flowers.'

She smiled at the flowers proudly and Jennifer swallowed. Supposing her mother did die. Jennifer didn't think she could bear it. Her mother had always been so indestructible. In a strange way, she was far more the linchpin of Jennifer's life than her father Edward. Sarah was the one she had hated, shouted at, resented, but all the time admired. Sarah was always at the centre of things. She always had friends. She was always on the phone to those in trouble while Jennifer and her father stood just watching, dreaming, musing, on the sidelines. But there was something of Sarah in Jennifer. At Cambridge she had flirted and teased as Sarah would have done. But she never did it as well as her mother because all the time, in the middle of a party, in a man's arms, being chased laughing across an expanse of lawn, she knew she wasn't quite there. Something indefinable was always missing. She looked for it in tranquillity, in drinking too much, in dancing, in affairs, even in churches. But she never seemed able to achieve the fullness of experience which her mother expected as her right.

'And tell me, how are you bearing up, Jenny?' said Sarah.

'It's taking me a long time to get over Martin.'

Sarah smoothed down her sheet severely. 'I've said it before and I'll say it again, you're better off without him, and the sooner you see that the better. He stifled you. Before you met him you were much more alive.'

Jennifer was amazed by her mother's vehemence and concern.

'I mean it, Jenny,' said Sarah firmly. 'You should have left him yourself.'

'I don't know,' said Jennifer, shaking her head. 'I love him. And I look at you and Edward together after all this time, and I think that perhaps he was the only one for you and you were the only one for him and that . . . I'm sorry . . . I didn't mean to say that . . . but sometimes I think Martin's, well, that he's the only one ever . . .'

Sarah's lips tensed. 'Edward's the only one I married, that's all, that's why he's important. There's you and the house and . . .'

'But it's not just that. I don't believe it's just that,' Jennifer said querulously. 'I'd like to think it was. I don't want to think you both wasted all those years without each other. It's just that when you're together . . . I don't know . . . I can't describe it . . . it's not the meeting of eyes or an explosion of sexual passion or anything like that. It's just that there's a kind of *rightness*... And that's what I feel with Martin.'

'Would you like a drink of something?' interrupted Sarah coolly, her eyes particularly bright. 'Lemonade perhaps? Shall I call the nurse?' She looked at her watch.

'Er, yes. Sorry. Yes, some lemonade would be smashing. I don't want to tire you. I must be going very soon.'

'Just stay another five minutes then... Nurse,' she shouted.

By Sarah's bedside was a pile of glossy magazines emblazoned with photographs of beautiful women and slashed with banners promising HEALTH AND BEAUTY.

'Let's hope it's not the gloomy nurse, the male one,' she said, examining her beautifully manicured nails. 'Mind you, if one has to be a nurse, and one's a male, I suppose it might make one a little glum. This one's a psychic type... like your Aunt Stella. Funny little boy. He keeps telling me not to worry about dying because I'll just be crossing over to the Other Side. What a great deal of nonsense they talk, these people. As far as I'm concerned, I'm alive and I'm staying that way. The "Other Side" might be a delightful place but I don't want to find out. If I want to talk to someone, I want to do so face to face in the here and now and not via some medium or some creaking chair.'

'Can I help you, Mrs Hamilton?' said a drab monotone.

Jennifer turned and her heart stiffened.

She and the male nurse stared at each other. 'It's Mike, isn't it?' she said.

For a moment it seemed he was going to deny it, and then he gave a grimace which was supposed to be a smile and said, 'Hello.' He was dressed in white tunic and trousers which accentuated the bloodless quality of his face.

'This is my mother,' said Jennifer.

'Ah, I see,' he said. 'What can I do for you, Mrs Hamilton?'

'Lemonade for us both, please.'

Sarah looked after him with dislike as he left the room. 'Where on earth did you meet that little creep?'

'At a friend's,' muttered Jennifer.

Sarah shrugged dismissively. 'I don't think much of your friends.'

'The friend is very understanding,' said Jennifer with a toss of her head. 'At present I need understanding friends.'

Sarah frowned. 'Look, Jenny, stop being so sorry for yourself. It's not so bad. What you have to remember is that you're not just one person. You're a number of them. With Martin, you'll always be one person; with someone else, you'll be a different one. Living with a new man is like...like reincarnation...you remember your past life with someone else, but not very clearly. Find yourself a new man. You're bloody lucky to have the opportunity. You can fight your way out of all this, as I can. My thirteen years alone have been terrific. I've had countless different lives within them. I've had innumerable men. It hasn't always been easy but I've been everywhere, done everything. I have lived. I haven't just existed, as most people do.'

'I don't want anyone but Martin,' said Jennifer.

'You will, you will. Go out, meet other men. The world never ends until you let it.'

'Men aren't the beginning and the end of things, you know,' said Jennifer fiercely. 'I can live without one, once I get used to it. I'd like to, as a matter of fact.'

'They make life a great deal easier for women. They admire us, provide for us, protect us. In return, we flatter them, organise them, have sex with them and spend their money.'

'I don't need looking after. I can manage.'

'You can't. You're too vulnerable. Not like me, as tough as old boots. Do stop glaring at me menacingly. I'm not applauding the power of men. But they've ruled for a long, long time now and we can't change it overnight.'

'Perhaps,' conceded Jennifer, staring at the wall behind Sarah and thinking what an unpleasant sheen it had, like the skin of Stephen Maugham. She was surrounded by strangeness. Nothing was real any more, not even her mother. It was not like her mother to be so warm.

'Of course, I made the mistake of living too hard, having too many affairs while I was married to Edward. I regretted it afterwards. But, my God, he was wet. He let me get away with it. Not like your Martin, who encouraged you to work so he could live it up with his students and his friends. That was quite different.'

'Not really,' said Jennifer. 'Edward wanted peace and quiet. He let you do as you pleased for the same reason I let Martin. To have some peace, some time alone. It was selfish behaviour on his part, not just on yours.'

Sarah looked shocked, and then her face lightened. 'I wish you'd told me that before,' she said. 'It would have been kind. I always blamed myself.'

'I'm sorry,' said Jennifer. 'It's something I have only understood recently.'

The door creaked open and Mike entered bearing a tray of lemonade and two glasses. He put the tray gently on the bedside as if he were planting a bomb. He then hurried away without a glance at either Jennifer or Sarah.

'What an awful person,' exclaimed Sarah. 'He looks like a genetic malfunction.'

'I must say I don't like him. He...' Jennifer was saying earnestly, when Edward entered the room and all the light in her mother's eyes turned to him.

Edward rushed over to kiss Sarah, hardly acknowledging Jennifer's presence.

'I have to go now,' said Jennifer.

'Oh, really?' said Edward, on the other side of the bed from Jennifer, looking at Sarah.

'Oh, Jenny, can't you stay a little longer?' said Sarah with her eyes on Edward.

'No, I really must go,' said Jennifer, feeling left out as she had felt left out all her childhood, out in the cold, hardly daring to knock.

At home that evening Jennifer walked in the garden. The flowers were all drooping from lack of water, the soil dry and crusty. Martin used to look after the garden, pick out the weeds, prune the roses, mow the lawn. In summer, on a Sunday, they

99

would sit outside and read the papers. And then, in the afternoon, he would play tennis and she would climb the stairs to her study and prepare the next day's lessons or work on her books. Books, books, books, bloody books and rooms and desks and windows looking out on places she could never get to. Children laughing in gardens all around. Lilac blossom she forgot to smell. People laughing and talking in carefree voices. Parties in the gardens of other houses, never her own.

All her life she had put off living until she had time to relax, until her work was done, until the moment was right. And now she was looking back in puzzlement at a life she hardly seemed to have lived. Perhaps her mother had had the right idea after all, she had grabbed every moment of pleasure, every sensation. But in the end, perhaps, it was all the same, at the end of life perhaps there is always puzzlement about where it all went, and regret.

12

'Honestly,' said Estelle the next day, brushing her frizzy hair with her hand and eyeing the boyish waiter appreciatively as his small bottom passed them by, 'at work there's hardly any man who isn't married and hardly any who are not also having an affair. They all do it. It's what people do nowadays. The men who don't appear to are only keeping the secret better or are uninterested in sex. Women just can't win. If you're a nice stay-at-home wife, the husband has it off with some glamorous career girl at work. Someone like me. And if you're not the domestic-bliss kind, he finds someone who will cook for him. Because really men want one of each. Quite understandable really. We live at a time of high expectations. Nobody wants to miss out on anything. Trouble is we women can't do the same thing, because it makes us miserable.'

Estelle and Jennifer were sitting in a Covent Garden wine bar watching the people go by. Everyone looked so very at ease with themselves as they swung their arms, giggled in the sunlight, walked with confident strides. Estelle was wearing a pair of pantaloons covered with yellow and white stars which made her look like a clown.

'I suppose you've just commissioned a book on infidelity, have you?' asked Jennifer.

'That's right,' said Estelle in a tone of surprise. '*Adulterous Sex*, it's going to be called, I'm afraid. By the way, how's your sex life?' she inquired, seizing a toothpick and proceeding to clean out her teeth. 'Are you getting on well with Richard?'

Jennifer shrugged. 'He phoned late last night, and I'm seeing him again this evening. We haven't had sex yet, if that's what you want to know.'

Jennifer had not been able to sleep last night after his phone call. It had seemed to her that there was someone in her room, although she could see no one. It had been the presence of a woman, cold and malevolent.

'Why would I want to know a private thing like that?' said Estelle, in mock hurt. She summoned the waiter. 'Two more glasses of wine please... Does he talk about his wife?' she asked, putting down the toothpick and leaning back, arms behind her head.

'A little.' Jennifer watched a chubby girl with a cocker-spaniel puppy trundle by with matching expressions of devotion as she looked down at him and he looked up at her. 'But what I really want to know I didn't like to ask,' continued Jennifer. 'Do you know how she killed herself?'

'Yes. She threw herself downstairs after dosing herself with drink and pills. Broke her neck. We should have ordered a bottle of the wine.'

Estelle crossed her legs. Everyone who went past goggled at her extraordinary pantaloons.

'Where was it that she fell?' asked Jennifer.

'I thought all this kind of thing distressed you,' said Estelle victoriously.

Jennifer flashed a steel smile at her friend. 'Estelle, where was it that she fell?'

Estelle uncrossed her legs and, with an air of retreat, took a sip of wine. 'Not sure,' she said. 'But the man who told me about it said that everyone was surprised he hadn't moved, so it must have happened in the same house he lives in now. The man's name is Rupert,' she continued wistfully. 'Lovely man he is. Works in the Home Office like Richard. But I married him off to Jane only a month ago.'

'What was she like?' asked Jennifer intently.

'Who? Jane?' Estelle reached in her handbag for a mirror and proceeded to apply lipstick in an infuriatingly nonchalant manner.

'Richard's wife,' snarled Jennifer.

Estelle finished applying her lipstick.

'Rupert said she was disdainful and rude but very pretty. I think she and Richard had awful rows and yet he adored her. Even now, people say, he won't change anything in his house because of her. It's all exactly as she left it. God knows why. Apparently at parties she was always putting him down and making eyes at other men. He's pretty attractive himself' — Estelle shot Jennifer that sly look — 'but he never had time for anyone but her.'

Jennifer experienced a moment of something she was surprised to note was jealousy.

Estelle put away her mirror and her lipstick.

'You know what I've been reading all morning? A book on the art of making party cakes. Party cakes, honestly. I went into publishing because I wanted to discover the next George Eliot, and all I discover is people who can describe how to make miniature railway engines out of pastry.' Estelle finished off her glass. She drinks too much, too often, thought Jennifer, with a rush of tenderness.

'Books, bloody hell,' continued Estelle, 'what a nuisance they are. Wish I'd never had an education. They've even ruined my love life. Do you know I always have to read two chapters before going to sleep? Whenever I drag some poor chap home for a night of love I always insist on reading my two chapters first. No wonder they don't come back. Anyway, I hate them using my bathroom in the morning.'

'We had two bathrooms,' said Jennifer, staring down at her own long white hands lying side by side on the red and blue checked tablecloth like two marble monuments.

'I *see*. So that's the secret of married life, is it?'

'And I often slept alone in the spare room when I was working late, which was most of the time. So I could read my two chapters then.'

'Oh well, at least we're both well read.'

Jennifer looked up and the two women grinned at each other.

'Jenny,' said Estelle, 'do you think you'll get married again?'

'God knows,' grunted Jennifer.

'You should. I don't recommend being single. All I want now is to get married and have children and be conventional.'

Estelle nodded at one of her publishing colleagues as he went by.

'Rubbish. If you actually wanted to marry, you would, instead of fixing up every available man with someone else.'

'Jennifer, you don't understand,' she said wearily. 'Men don't want to marry me because I'm not quiet and demure like women should be. The ones who do like intelligent, liberated women are usually gay anyway. The rest can't cope with people like me. And what is really unfair is that in the end what we want is what women have always wanted: a home and some children. I do! I want that. Babies and cooking and security.' She leant back further in her chair, the sun on her face. 'I wasn't warned. I didn't know I'd want all that.'

'I keep saying that about the breakdown of my marriage,' said Jennifer, keen to reintroduce the subject. 'About not being warned.'

'Huh. You're all right,' continued Estelle, sitting up straight. 'You've already got another man after you. There's something quite demure about you, there always was. You always look so innocent and serious. You used to stand behind me staring out with your big green eyes and all the men headed for you.'

'What nonsense. You had countless boyfriends. They never left you alone.'

'But they fell in love with you,' said Estelle solemnly.

'Nonsense,' said Jennifer. 'I spent all my time working.'

Estelle raised her eyebrows. 'You were easily as wild as me when it suited you. You think of yourself as quiet and shy but you're not, you know. I've seen you in rages. I've seen you jealous. You're scared stiff of the violence of your emotions, that's your trouble.'

'Estelle, why don't you run a problem page or become a psychiatrist instead of doling out all this advice and analysis for free?'

'Well, I just wish you'd be more honest with yourself,' said Estelle. 'For one thing, your books are full of exhortations to women to be free and now you sit around whining about your marriage.'

'It's not just my marriage. I feel I have put ordinary human values in second place, below achievement. I have neglected friends as well as Martin.'

'Well, I'm glad to hear I'm about to get more attention.' She brightened. 'Shall we go and visit Sheila in her toy shop? I'd like to do that. I'm fond of your friend Sheila. We met in the street yesterday and I truly think she's in a worse state than either of us, which might be comforting for us both.' They grinned at each other, the old camaraderie of Cambridge returning.

Estelle insisted on paying the bill and they sauntered off together, Estelle a bizarre sight in white tee shirt, frizzy hair, glasses and the pantaloons, Jennifer more ordinary in jeans and a man's shirt, one of Martin's.

As they walked into the market a man stood playing the clarinet to a crowd of pigeons and a few tourists. The cheery tune reminded her that things weren't really so bad.

A giant pottery tiger stood guard over one window, another window displayed a pair of black and gold boots for £150, a third contained embroidered waistcoats and a fourth specialised in body lotions. The word 'market', a hangover from the days of the old fruit and vegetable market, was not a very apt description of this collection of chic, expensive shops, brightly painted with a deceptive innocence. The only market stalls were in the central arcade, and they were far from cheap. But as the clarinet music continued to float through the air, a curious magic came over the arcade. For a moment it seemed that everyone had frozen in position — an old lady leaning forward for a bracelet, a man touching the silk of a nightdress, a market stallholder with her hands on her hips. It was as though they were about to burst into the song and dance of a musical.

Estelle and Jennifer moved away, down to the lower level of the market, and into the toy shop. It was busy with dragon puppets, princess puppets, action men, computer games and cuddly animals including a huge pink pig feeding three little piglets.

105

Earnest children were informing their parents how much they liked that train set, or that model car, while less cunning younger ones announced, 'I want that.' The very young ones just grabbed at what they wanted.

'Jenny!' cried Sheila. 'I'll be with you in one minute.' She was talking to a bearded young man, who wore jeans and a shirt with an air of casual confidence. He had a leather bag over his shoulder. Jennifer envied Sheila for working in such a bustling, companionable place as Covent Garden.

Sheila hurried towards them and greeted them both with a kiss. As usual, she looked half-child herself, with her fragile face, pudgy lips and fair hair. In a brightly striped tee shirt and a tight blue skirt above long legs, she reminded Jennifer of a young deer. At the nearest wine bar, on the pavement, in the sun, watching the people, Sheila informed Jennifer that she had left her husband.

'Now what I want to know is, have I done the right thing? You know us both. What do you think? I want to approach this whole thing calmly.' Sheila was such an emotional girl that it was curious to see her trying so hard to be rational.

'I'm not sure,' said Jennifer.

'I've moved to his house — Brian's house — in Chelsea. And I keep thinking everything's fine, of course I've made the right decision, and then I burst into tears. The awful thing is, you see, or maybe it's not awful, the awful thing is that he didn't mind. Tim didn't seem to mind at all. That made it clear to me why I'd had the affair. He obviously didn't love me. I wanted to be loved, I needed it. He hadn't loved me for months. But what I feel is — and I know this sounds silly — but I think I love Tim very deeply. And now it's too late. Do you think it's too late?'

'I just don't know,' said Jennifer.

'Good grief, it's only been two days,' said Estelle, lighting up a cigarette. 'You really mustn't panic.'

'I am in love with Brian, there's no doubt about that,' said Sheila, brushing her hair from her face with a bewildered expression. 'But does that mean I should spend the rest of my life with him?'

106

'Nope,' said Estelle. 'It doesn't even mean you're compatible. But it's a good start.'

'Of course you're upset now,' said Jennifer. 'Even if you loathed your husband, it would be natural to be upset. You've just got to live through it, and see how you feel once you're more peaceful.'

Sheila pushed back her hair again and Jennifer experienced her desperation. It was strange to her how open she was to other people's emotions now.

'I think you have no idea what's going on, and the best idea would be to take a long holiday alone to sort yourself out,' said Estelle.

'But it is too late. I think it is. He says it's all over.' Sheila was staring straight in front of her with a peculiar smile. 'One person said that if I decided to try to return to him, I should just write "I love you" on a piece of paper and send it to him. Another said I should just withdraw completely out of his life, a third that I should go away somewhere and work out exactly why he fell in love with me in the first place and then arrange some casual meeting and show off those qualities. What do you think?'

Jennifer was amazed by Sheila's strategies. It was as though her problem was a mathematical one with a solution. There was something endearing and pathetic about such an illogical person trying to impose logic on the horror of losing someone she loved.

Sheila twitched her head every now and again as she spoke. She was trying to remain calm and her intonations made what she said sound perfectly reasonable. She was pretending to be in command of the situation. She was pretending that she wasn't panicking.

Jennifer was too confused herself to know what advice to give, but she did know she was afraid for Sheila.

'You must try to keep calm,' she said. 'I'm sure Tim will have you back if you want him to. Just try to stop worrying.'

She looked at Jennifer pleadingly. 'Do you really think he'd take me back?'

'Of course. He always seemed very fond of you.'

Sheila's features lightened a little. 'Really?'

'Oh yes,' said Jennifer, with what she hoped was a reassuring smile. In fact Tim had not seemed especially fond of Sheila. They had been married for five years and he appeared to take her for granted.

'You know what I think?' said Estelle, lighting a cigarette. 'I think we're all far too keen on maintaining our own identities. It gets us nowhere. It means that you and Jennifer haven't changed along with your partners — haven't become wives really — and therefore you probably do need new partners for new stages of life, or they do, anyway. You've probably done the right thing in the circumstances. As for me, I've maintained my own identity so well that no man will come within a mile of me.'

'I don't know what that's got to do with me,' said Sheila plaintively. 'My problem is that I fell in love with Brian and yet I love Tim. I love them both! You know, I'm addicted to Brian,' she confided, moving closer to Jennifer and Estelle, away from the group of businessmen at a nearby table who were staring at the girls with interest. 'That's the problem. If I don't see him for a day or two, I'm in agony. I tried to give him up but I couldn't, and yet in leaving Tim I seem to have wandered out of my life into someone else's and I can't make any sense of it. Of course I should have kept them both going, but how could I have done that to Tim?'

'Shall we have something to eat?' said Estelle, a little fed up. 'I'm starving.'

'I really couldn't,' said Sheila, brushing her hair from her face again.

'Well, I shall.' She summoned the waiter authoritatively. He smiled at Jennifer as she and Estelle ordered, while Sheila waited impatiently to start talking again. All Jennifer and Sheila wanted to do was to talk and talk in the hope that at the end of all the talking they would understand better what was going on in their minds and in their hearts. Sheila's brow was furrowed. She did seem very close to the edge where Jennifer herself was standing.

Her pale eyes blinked emptily. 'It's just that Brian was pulling so hard and Tim wasn't pulling back and so I fell into Brian's arms.

He wants me so much, Jenny. That's the problem. And I do love him more than I've ever loved anyone before.'

'What are you worrying about then?' asked Jennifer.

'You should take a holiday,' repeated Estelle.

'I just can't bear the thought of this amount of pain continuing,' said Sheila. 'I've given up stability for passion and, although I was perfectly able to live without passion, I don't think I can live without stability. I can't stand it.'

It was essential, Jennifer told Sheila, to concentrate on just one day at a time, cope with only twenty-four hours of chaos. Once one began to look into the future, the bleak prospect of endless days of misery was impossible to bear. Tomorrow, anything can happen, she said; there'll be other men, other houses, other dreams.

'Good Lord, girl,' said Estelle to Sheila. 'It's only been two days. You've just left your husband. Of course you're upset. Take some tranquillisers. Take a holiday. Relax. You've got a lover you adore who adores you. Things aren't so terrible,' she added, a little bitterly.

'And everyone has been very kind, very kind indeed,' said Sheila. 'Do you know, even one of the toy salesmen was sympathetic? He looked at my face this morning and he knew at once something was wrong. Isn't that extraordinary? He sells toys because he loves children and loves to see their little faces light up.' She stared dreamily into the distance. 'Brian and I are thinking of having a child.'

'I thought you were thinking of leaving him,' snorted Estelle.

She sighed. 'I am.'

'Honestly. You're in love. Pull yourself together,' said Estelle. 'Enjoy it.'

'What's the name of this toy salesman?' asked Jennifer quietly.

'Stephen Maugham,' said Sheila. 'He's weird. But very understanding. And do you know he's asked me to lunch...' She put her hand to her mouth. 'Oh dear... today.' She glanced at her watch. 'I'm late.' She jumped up.

'I've met him,' said Jennifer flatly.

'He's odd, isn't he? A real character,' exclaimed Sheila.

Before Jennifer could reply, Sheila had hurried off through the crowds towards the restaurant, swinging her straw bag in an excess of nervous energy until she was lost from view.

'She's lovely, isn't she?' said Estelle.

'Yes, she is,' said Jennifer, and suddenly felt very worried about her indeed. 'Poor thing.'

For the rest of the day she couldn't settle down. One minute she was worrying about Sheila and the next about her mother's operation on the following day. She jumped every time the phone rang.

She switched on the television at five o'clock and was relieved to see other people talking. The television programme gave off a bright light, like a Christmas tree. What she wanted was reassurance, trivia and ordinariness. She wanted to concentrate on the little things of life so that she did not have to see the big things. That was the trick, that was how people stopped themselves from falling. Gossiping with old friends, deciding whether or not to have foam in one's bath, taking the dog for a walk, reading magazines, counting the money in one's purse.

She called Sheila. She was out.

She called Estelle. She was out.

She called three other friends.

Eventually she called Richard. The line was engaged. She phoned again.

'How funny,' he said. 'I was just calling you.' His voice sounded so warm that for a while the blackness withdrew.

'Can I come round a little earlier than we arranged? About seven?'

'Yes, yes please,' said Jennifer.

13

As she dressed to go out with Richard she heard a drumming on the window. It was spattered with rain. She opened it wide and took a deep breath of the fresh wet air. The colours of the trees and the flowers were already brighter, cleaner, the rain washing away the dust which seemed to have covered everything these last few hot weeks.

The lupins stood proud and purple and the roses rambled over the wall while the ivy shone with patches of white as though hit by moonbeams. The regretful, hopeful fragrance of honeysuckle breathed out as the trees creaked and the leaves rustled. At least it was all still there, all that beauty, the cobwebs, the hints and memories waiting for her in the shades of a rose.

When the doorbell rang she did not want to answer it. She felt tranquil. And when she did she tensed at the sight of the grave, stooping figure with the raindrops sparkling in his grey hair, bringing with him the world of men, taking away her moments of peace.

'I'll just get my coat,' she gasped.

'Aren't you going to invite me in?' he murmured reproachfully. 'It's awfully wet out here.'

'Of course. Of course. Come in.'

He entered the hall wearing the same tweed jacket as before, but now with one button missing, and what looked like the same shirt with a frayed collar. He peered round with a mixture of furtiveness and gawkiness.

'What a big house,' he remarked.

'I'll have to move soon,' she explained and scuttled off towards the kitchen. He followed her. 'It's too big for me, you see.' She spun round. 'Have a drink.'

'How charming of you to offer.'

She shot him a quick glance. Was he mocking her? A slight smile was edging up his face.

On her way to the fridge she bumped into a chair. The rain was drumming on the roof of the kitchen. He was watching her. She wished he'd say something, anything. He was standing close to her and took the bottle from her, watching her as he did so.

'The corkscrew!' she exclaimed. 'Where is it?'

He picked it up from the table and proceeded to open the bottle.

'Glasses! I'll get the glasses.' The glasses were washed but still cloudy. Martin had always complained about her inability to provide gleaming glasses. I can write books, she thought, as she washed two of the goblets which had been wedding presents, I can teach children, but what else can I do? Richard took the glasses from her, dried them, all in silence as outside the leaves rustled in the rain.

'What's the matter?' he asked her gently as he gave her some wine and she took it with trembling hands.

'Nothing,' she said.

Richard's closeness now reminded her of his closeness in the cinema. He was watching her inquisitively. 'Have you seen Mrs Maugham again?' he asked.

She nodded.

'And Stephen?'

'Yes, he was there too.'

'What do you think of him?'

'I think he's loathsome.'

Their bodies were very near to each other and hers was swaying slightly.

'Apparently he is very attractive to women. Do you find him attractive?'

Richard was leaning over her.

She shook her head. 'I told you, I think he's loathsome.'

'That's what my wife said but she was drawn to him. She talked about him and Mrs Maugham all the time, she thought about them all the time, she couldn't stop seeing them. She said once that Stephen Maugham had the attraction of evil.'

'I don't know what you're talking about,' said Jennifer, although she did, and she was afraid for Sheila even now, as she stood in the darkened kitchen and heard the cry of cats fighting together somewhere out there, among the bushes and the trees and the dark shapes of the deserted gardens. Put your arms around me and tell me not to be afraid, Richard, please, tell me it's all in my mind, tell me these horrors are not really there, tell me I'm just a foolish young woman, tell me Sheila will come to no harm, that I will come to no harm, that my mother's illness does not exist, that time and death and loss are not all around us, in the rain and in the darkness and the silence of this room full of memories.

'You're shivering,' he said tenderly.

She smiled. 'It's cold.'

'Perhaps you'd better get yourself a sweater,' he said, and his eyes meandered over her thin silk blouse. Confused, embarrassed, reddening, she did up the top button. Underneath was a white lacy bra and it seemed to Jennifer that he could see that, and that he could see her silk knickers and the softness of her belly and the roundness of her breasts.

'Are you going to see them again?' he murmured soothingly as though inviting her to tell him the truth.

'Who?'

He stiffened. 'You know perfectly well who,' he snapped. 'You look up at me with those innocent eyes, like my wife used to do. And all the while you're planning to see them again, aren't you? You won't take any notice of me.' He gripped her shoulders. 'What is it about them? Do you want to end up dead like your aunt, like my wife, like two of Stephen's wives, like Mrs Maugham's husband? Is that what you want?'

'Sometimes,' she said, quietly.

'They are dangerous people, Jennifer. Very dangerous indeed. Believe me, I know.'

'What exactly are you saying, Richard?'

113

Lines furrowed his forehead, and for a moment he looked quite old, although his eyes were still young, and they were pleading with her.

'Can't you just believe me? I... I'm unable to tell you everything. It just isn't possible. I'd like to... but I can't.'

'Mrs Maugham told me that the death of your wife had made you paranoid.'

He let go of her, his hands falling hopelessly to his sides. 'And you believe that, do you?' he said.

'I don't know. I don't know you. Why do you have to talk about all this? I thought we were going out. I thought we were going out for a nice, merry evening. I don't want to stand here in this dark, cold kitchen talking about death.'

'Well, you're a very silly girl then.' His eyes snarled at her. 'My wife was silly too. She wouldn't face up to what was happening to her.'

Jennifer shrugged irritatingly. 'Nothing is happening to me. I've just paid two visits to a rather friendly old woman who turns out to be far more understanding than anyone else I've come across in a long while. And I need someone understanding. It's true, I'm a little weak at the moment. It's true that in normal circumstances I would not be confiding in Mrs Maugham. But these are not normal circumstances. I've never felt more abnormal.'

'But that's exactly it. That's why she's got under your skin.'

Jennifer smiled. '"Under my skin" — that's ridiculous. You make it sound as though I'm suffering from some adolescent infatuation with the old girl.'

'Don't laugh at me, Jennifer.'

'Then please stop being so intense and humourless.'

'I think I'd better go.'

Don't go, she thought, please don't go and leave me here in this house all alone. Please. Something is happening. I'm scared. Stay with me. Or take me out, to somewhere brightly lit. Be ordinary, cheerful, flirt with me. Say I'm pretty, hold my hand, make me drunk.

'Fine, if you want to go,' she said.

'I will go. I don't want to bore you any more.'

At the front door, he turned to her. 'I just want to take up a few moments more of your valuable time before you phone up someone else to take you out somewhere "merry" where you can show off that nicely made-up face of yours, and that very pretty blouse, and...' She wanted him to kiss her, but she was angry too, angry at the way he was looking her up and down, watching her slender legs flow up to her skirt, and the skirt to her blouse, soft against her skin, angry at the desire for him which made her long to grab his arm and tell him not to go, please not to leave her like this...

'I just want to tell you one or two things which happened to my wife. It might be worth your bearing them in mind.'

Stop being so pompous, stop being so far away from me, stop holding your head up like that, stop it now. I can't cope with it. My mother may be dying. Her operation is tomorrow. Don't be like this. You know that we need each other. You know you care about me. You wouldn't be so angry if you didn't care. Please stop it.

'My wife, as I believe I mentioned to you, was a very listless person. There was nothing she cared about. She claimed she had been depressed all her life. For a while, when we were first in love, she was quite different: cheerful, perhaps a little too cheerful, perhaps there was something manic in her high spirits, I don't know. But after a year or two she changed. She moped around the house. And occasionally, just occasionally, she would have fits of destruction. That was usually after seeing Mrs Maugham. I did my best to cope with it. But, as you've perhaps gathered, I am not an especially secure person myself. I found her behaviour bewildering and disturbing, and sometimes it made me angry. It wasn't that she occasionally threw something at me during a row, behaviour you would no doubt think very reasonable. It wasn't like that. Are you listening to me? Your eyes are blank. Listen.' How arrogant and sad he was. There were shadows under his eyes. 'What she really wanted was to destroy herself, she said, but of

115

course — I didn't believe her, didn't think she was that kind of person. Listen to me. She said she hated herself, hated me, and hated being alive. Anything would trigger off one of her fits — an angry word from me, a bad day at work, a distressing item on the news. She would go round the house smashing things or she would take the car out. Once she crashed it but luckily escaped alive. Three times she was up for speeding offences. She used to say that at the moment of destruction — the moment the glass smashes onto the floor, the moment the looking-glass breaks — at that moment, she said, all the fragments of her personality came together and she was completely herself.'

It was as though a gale were blowing through Jennifer and she could hardly stand.

'Stop it, Richard. I don't want to know.'

'Of course you don't. That isn't the point. But it is important that you do.' He was standing very close to her. Their bodies were almost touching. 'At least then I will have done my best as I didn't do my best before,' he said more softly. 'She used to say that the desire to destroy oneself is as strong as any creative urge — not that she had creative urges. She used to think what bliss it would be to take all those pills, drive one's car into a tree, cut one's wrists. Destruction is a form of self-expression, she used to say. Like Cleopatra killing herself, or Mark Antony, people who completed their own lives like a painter finished a painting. But really, until she met Mrs Maugham, all these feelings remained unformulated. Mrs Maugham made her really believe there was something noble about suicide. She encouraged her to kill herself.'

'Don't be ridiculous,' said Jennifer. The rain had stopped. Suddenly the house was still.

'Little by little she won the confidence of my wife and then she and Stephen Maugham together set about making her kill herself.'

Richard seemed very far away, back in the past.

'I think all this has been too much for you,' said Jennifer.

'And don't forget Stephen,' he said with sudden urgency. 'He appears to be under her control, but I'm not too sure. Her interest is in manipulation and power, power over life and death. She sees herself as a female God, in contact with the dead and the living, moving people from one state to the other like a chess player. He is in some ways more dangerous because he is more human.'

Now Jennifer really did want Richard to go, at once. She saw Sheila's face in her mind, innocent, open, vulnerable, and she saw Stephen Maugham too, always amused, watching with those thin eyes, his tongue running over his rubbery lips, his yellow skin shining. She did not want to think about them, she did not want to know about the horror and the guilt and the blame which were seething in Richard's mind, making him mad. She was sure he was mad, he had to be mad.

'If you really think this, why don't you go to the police?' she asked, fumbling to open the door for him to go.

'I can't do that,' he said, and loped off into the night without even saying goodbye.

She stood there, at the door, the darkness inside her deepening, and she felt the chill of despair.

There was a van parked on the other side of the street. For a moment she felt quite sure that the man in the van was Stephen Maugham, although she could not see his face, which was turned away. She shut the door at once, her heart beating very fast.

She called Estelle, who came over at once, and together they went out to dinner. By that time the van had gone.

That night Jennifer had bad dreams and awoke with a scream at five o'clock after seeing Stephen Maugham standing over her with a knife. She fell asleep and dreamt of Sheila lying ashen-faced on a bed, one arm hanging lifelessly over the edge.

She tossed and turned until, at nine o'clock, she got up and called Sheila's new number, Brian's number. But there was no reply. She called Tim, Sheila's husband, but there was no reply there either. She wandered over the house restlessly, thinking about her mother, praying for her mother, afraid for Sheila. Still in her nightdress, she re-arranged some flowers on the kitchen table, ate half a strawberry yoghurt, glanced at the newspapers and brushed her teeth again and again and again but they still looked a little yellow to her, like the teeth of Stephen Maugham. The cotton nightdress clung to the sweat on her back.

She decided to go over and see her father. At least they could be together today, the day of Sarah's operation; at least she might be of some comfort to him.

14

As Jennifer passed the house of Sheila and Tim, she rang the doorbell. She waited for some time but nobody came to the door. A black cat watched her from the windowsill with cool, appraising eyes. She rang the bell again. All the curtains were drawn, as though the house had closed its eyes on the world.

It was a subdued, drizzly morning. The sky hung low over the grey street, which was veiled in a mist of cold rain. Jennifer wrapped her scarf more tightly around her and rang the bell for a third time. A car swished by.

She walked off, not looking behind her, towards the main street mushrooming with umbrellas, towards newsagents' and traffic lights and brightly lit food shops. It is all in my imagination, she told herself, hailing a taxi which she directed not to her father's house but to 23 Reynolds Walk.

Jennifer's hands were trembling when Lily ushered her through the hall and into the main room, where all the stuffed animals turned their startled eyes onto her.

Lily took up position behind Mrs Maugham's armchair like a nurse. She looked more stern than she had the last time.

The windows were shaking a little in the wind and the room was dark except for the faint light of one table lamp. The dying chrysanthemums on the coffee table reminded her of her visit to the spiritualist church.

'My dear!' said Mrs Maugham. 'My goodness, you look wan. Do sit down and take a chocolate. Now, how are you?'

Lily stared at Jennifer with a gentle smile and glazed eyes. She wore a white blouse and blue pleated skirt, from which her legs stuck out like sticks. Her mousy hair hung down straight on either side of her thin anaemic face.

'Not too good.' Jennifer sat down a little self-consciously on the sofa, disturbed by Lily's gaze.

Mrs Maugham lifted her feet onto her embroidered footstool. 'Tell me everything. Heavens! I do hate to see anyone miserable!' There were deep pink flowers printed over Mrs Maugham's black forties-style dress. Her lipstick matched the pink.

'Well,' said Jennifer, 'I wondered if I could perhaps have a sitting. My mother's having her operation this afternoon.'

Mrs Maugham smiled, sending out warmth and sympathy from the expression on her lips and in her eyes. 'My dear,' she said softly. 'I'm sorry. As if you haven't enough to bear.'

'Are you going to give her a sitting?' asked Lily.

'Yes, my dear. Of course,' she murmured. She stretched out for a chocolate. 'Lily, be an angel and close the curtains, could you?'

Jennifer moved restlessly on her seat.

'Now be calm, my dear. We must all relax. We must relax and clear our minds of all unnecessary worries and thoughts. We must have peaceful and receptive minds for the spirits to come to us. Now, Lily dearest, stand still, won't you? If you are receptive, perhaps we will receive a message from the Other Side.'

'Jennifer could pick up a message herself if she chose,' intoned Lily. 'I can feel it. She is one of us, Mrs Maugham. I like Jennifer.'

'Heavens! Yes, yes, dear, I know that. Now do be peaceful, my dear. Do try not to talk. The spirits are gathering around. I can feel their presence. They are not speaking clearly but I know that they wish to give you a message, Jennifer.'

'Why don't you let Jennifer make contact?' said Lily, looking at the hummingbird.

'Do be quiet, Lily,' said Mrs Maugham firmly. 'You're spoiling my concentration.' Mrs Maugham closed her eyes and turned her palms upwards. Lily was staring at Jennifer with interest.

After a few minutes of silence, Mrs Maugham began to speak. 'I have a young girl here...oh!' Mrs Maugham lurched slightly. 'An impact. Do you recognise this? Do you know someone who was killed in a crash?'

'Yes. A schoolfriend was knocked off her bicycle and killed.'

'Ah.' Mrs Maugham kept her eyes closed. 'Jennifer, you must relax. Your mind keeps getting busy.'

'I'm sorry.'

'She says you must take care.'

Jennifer nodded.

'She was a lovely girl, wasn't she? But not happy.'

Jennifer nodded again.

'She says she's happy now. She's peaceful at last. It's very calm on the Other Side. There's no friction, no confusion,' she said.

Lily's eyes were still intent on Jennifer's face.

'She was very fond of you and she doesn't like to see you suffering,' continued Mrs Maugham. 'But she wants you to know she is watching you and wanting to help. She is waiting for you, she says. She is holding out her arms to you in affection. She has been there on the Other Side for a long, long time and wants you to know that she wishes you well.'

'And she says your mother will be all right,' said a different, gentler voice. It was Lily's.

Jennifer opened her eyes wide and saw irritation flit across Mrs Maugham's face as Lily smiled at Jennifer sympathetically and made her feel strong. 'She keeps saying that your mother will live. Your friend knows too — that it will be all right,' said Lily. 'Her name was Rebecca, wasn't it?'

'Yes,' said Jennifer. 'It was.'

'That's very good, Lily,' said Mrs Maugham a touch tartly. 'But please, dear, try not to interrupt me. I was just about to come to that part of the message.'

'Sorry,' said Lily stiffly.

'Perhaps you had better pull back the curtains, dear,' said Mrs Maugham to Lily, stretching out for a comforting chocolate. 'I don't think I could work now.' She wiped her perspiring brow with her large handkerchief. 'I do so hate being interrupted.'

Lily pulled back the curtains. It was as grey and dismal outside as it was in.

'You'd better be off now and do the shopping,' said Mrs Maugham to Lily, who looked sulky. 'We need some food for lunch.'

Lily gathered up her large coat from the back of the sofa and said goodbye to them both. She smiled at Jennifer. 'Don't worry,' she said as she left. 'It really is all for the best.'

'She's in a difficult mood today, I'm afraid,' Mrs Maugham said after she'd gone. 'You know, she works in a chemist shop in Victoria Street but still lives at home in Surrey because she's afraid of London. Heavens! It's a terrible burden to see more than others can see. But she'll be a great medium one day, mark my words, although at times she can be a little too soft-hearted. Now, my dear, do you feel any better?'

'Much better,' said Jennifer. 'You've been very kind.'

'There's something else on your mind though, isn't there?'

Jennifer nodded. 'A friend of mine. Sheila Humphreys. She knows your brother.'

Mrs Maugham's hands went up to the pearls around her neck while her expression remained the same: sympathetic, interested, kindly. 'Heavens! I think it's sweet of you to be so concerned for a friend when your mother's so ill and you're so unhappy yourself. Tell me. How do you feel? Are things any less painful for you, my dear?'

'I don't know. At the moment I can't stop thinking about Sheila. I wondered if I should ask her to come to see you.'

'Certainly,' said Mrs Maugham.

'She's left her husband for her lover, you see, Mrs Maugham, and now she regrets it or thinks she does. But the real problem seems to be that she loves them both.'

Jennifer's brow was creased as she leant confidingly close to Mrs Maugham. 'Please, Mrs Maugham,' said Jennifer, 'please do try to help her if you can.'

'Of course. Why of course, my dear,' said Mrs Maugham,

looking down as she spread the flowery dress over her ample knees. 'But until I've met her you are my chief concern.'

'You are kind, Mrs Maugham, terribly kind... And, well, there's something else disturbing me... your brother. You know, I dreamed of your brother last night.'

'Keep away from my brother,' said Mrs Maugham.

'Why? What are you suggesting, Mrs Maugham?'

Mrs Maugham smiled. 'I suggest nothing. Nothing at all. I live half in and half out of life. Who am I to suggest? I exist in the twilight.' She drew closer to Jennifer. 'Dear girl. Do take care.'

'I'm fine.'

Mrs Maugham regarded her with such sympathy that Jennifer longed to be in her arms, enfolded, safe, smothered in the powder and scent and pillowing breasts.

'Poor Jenny. Life is such a torment for you, isn't it, my dear? So very difficult. You have a glow in your cheeks now but in your heart you know it's only temporary, don't you?' Mrs Maugham reached for a chocolate and then offered the box to Jennifer. 'Now take the orange cream. It's delicious and it'll do you good.' She moved her bottom on the sofa. 'What I really want to know is whether or not you wish to join our little group and spread the word. We need someone of your looks and intelligence, someone who can mix with ordinary people and important people. Stephen, Lily, myself... as I said, well, we're a little eccentric for that kind of thing.' Mrs Maugham mopped her brow again. 'Now, tell me, have you considered your future with us?'

'No,' said Jennifer.

'My dear, I have your interests at heart. You should turn to spiritualism for comfort. You have great powers, my dear. You could become one of us.'

'What does that mean?'

'I think you should join our little circle. Chiefly, we help to alleviate the fear of passing over. We make people look forward to passing from this world to the next. But I'd advise you first to cut off all contact with that Richard Stevenson. As I say, he's dangerous.'

'I'll think about it,' said Jennifer flatly.

Mrs Maugham eased herself up and went over to the mantel-piece above the empty fireplace. She stroked the glossy head of the black raven.

'As one of us, you would have power, Jennifer, my dear. You would commune with the spirits who watch human beings play out their tragedies and farces. You would be able to control fates, relieve suffering, be more than just a puppet or a prisoner in the condemned cell of life. Think about it, my dear, certainly. But think about it very seriously.'

Mrs Maugham got her shawl from the back of the armchair. 'Your husband has clamped you down for a while, but you can't remain clamped down for ever. You've always been different and you always will be. You can pretend to be ordinary, of course. But that won't *make* you ordinary.' Mrs Maugham wrapped the shawl around her shoulders. 'I'd rather you didn't come back here to see me until you have made a decision one way or another. Your indecision distresses me. You do understand, my dear, what I'm saying, don't you?' She was staring at Jennifer with her hard blue eyes.

'I think so,' said Jennifer, shivering and thinking how very large and imposing Mrs Maugham seemed when she wasn't sitting down. She was aware that she was being punished and wondered how on earth she would be able to get through the next few days without Mrs Maugham's support.

Mrs Maugham kissed Jennifer when she left for her father's house, and Jennifer went on her way feeling as desolate as if she'd kissed goodbye to a lover.

15

At Edward's house later that day, the phone rang while her father was making coffee and Jennifer was sitting in his study's big leather swivel chair, waiting for the news from the hospital and thinking about her mother.

She let Edward answer the phone. As she waited, swaying her chair back and forth, she stared at three photographs side by side on Edward's desk: Sarah, black-haired, vivacious, smiling out of the past; beside her, Jennifer, in school uniform with the familiar urchin grin and avid green eyes, looking very much her mother's daughter; Edward, grey-haired, unsmiling. Jennifer knew that Edward and Sarah needed each other, and that she needed them.

'Jenny!' yelled Edward. 'It's for you.'

'Jenny? Estelle here. Have you heard?' Estelle's voice sounded very peculiar.

'Not yet. The operation must still be going on.'

'What are you talking about? I'm talking about Sheila, Sheila Humphreys.'

'What about her?' said Jennifer, knowing with a sudden kick of horror what Estelle was about to say.

'She's killed herself.'

A few minutes later Jennifer left the house for Tim's. On the way, she saw three people she thought were Stephen Maugham. I'm going crazy, she told herself. My imagination is driving me crazy.

As Tim opened the door, Jennifer at once felt the silence and the emptiness. He seemed to be tilting forwards like the leaning tower of Pisa and his eyes were huge in his chalky, freckly face.

'I'm sorry,' said Jennifer, putting her arms around him. 'I really am most terribly sorry.'

He was still sobbing half an hour later as she made him a cup of tea surrounded by the watching cats. It was getting darker but they didn't think to switch on the lights. The air was heavy with the probability of rain. The cats were whining for some milk.

'She smelt of whisky. And I thought, this can't be. She can't be ending up like this.' He shook his head. 'If only she'd known just how sordid suicide is. There's nothing to admire in a dead body and a white empty face. It was horrible, Jenny, absolutely horrible.'

He was shaking his head as if seeing what he had seen earlier in the day, when he had returned home from work at lunchtime to pick up some things he had forgotten and discovered her body naked on the bed with an empty pill bottle and a half-drunk bottle of whisky beside her.

The tabby cat jumped on Jennifer's lap and Jennifer stroked her again and again and began to cry.

Sheila had let herself into the house with her own key after Tim had gone to work. The police said she must have died at about twelve, shortly before Tim had dropped by. He called an ambulance at once, but it was too late.

'I can't imagine how she could have been so stupid,' he said. 'She'd never threatened suicide. Not once. I wouldn't have thought she was the type. I mean, she wasn't someone who frequently got depressed. Most of the time she was so cheerful. I know that she was upset about what had happened, but it was no reason to do that. I wasn't to know, surely? I never even suspected. You wouldn't have thought she was that type of person, would you?'

'No,' said Jennifer, and blew her nose loudly. The cat jumped off her lap and ran to the door.

'You'd have thought she'd have at least threatened it once, wouldn't you?' said Tim. 'You'd have thought she'd have given some warning? Isn't that what people usually do? Oh Christ, what a horrible way to die. Soon my parents will be coming round and taking me back to their house in Richmond for a few days and when I return she'll still be dead.'

He put his head in his hands. 'The police asked me questions, about our relationship. I couldn't bear it. The body was taken away. It was all so dingy, the suicide. Really not at all how you'd think. Much dingier, more horrible.'

'Could you go abroad for a while? You should get away from this house,' said Jennifer. She moved closer to him and stroked his hair soothingly. Then she slipped her arm round his shoulders.

'If only I'd realised just how upset she was,' he said in a throttled voice. 'But how could I have guessed she'd do this? It never entered my mind. I still can't believe it's happened.'

'You couldn't have guessed. Nobody could have. It's not your fault at all. You must not blame yourself. Anyway, it might have been an accident.'

'When she told me about her lover, I wasn't surprised,' said Tim, staring at Jennifer vacantly. 'I'd guessed she was having an affair for months but had thought it would blow over. Plenty of people have affairs. They aren't necessarily important. It was when she said that she wanted to leave that I couldn't bear it. You can understand that, can't you? I just wanted her out of the house, immediately, at once. I couldn't stand to see her sitting there, so pretty, her hair all fluffy from having been just washed, and know that she belonged to someone else. She left with just a suitcase. But she was weeping when she left and asking shouldn't we start again, and I said no, that was impossible now. I wanted to hurt her. Of course I did. She'd hurt me so much. That's natural, isn't it? But that night I woke up and when I realised she wasn't in the bed beside me I went looking for her in every room of the house, calling her name. It was stupid. I must have been sleepwalking. I felt so silly when I remembered that she'd gone.'

'Have you spoken to the man... to Brian?'

'Oh yes. I called him. They had his number at the shop. He said they'd had a bad quarrel. She must have been angry, mustn't she, to do something like this? She must have wanted to punish me and him and somehow got the idea of suicide into her diseased mind.

It must have been diseased, mustn't it? Nobody sane would do something like this?'

'I suppose not,' said Jennifer.

'Brian was stunned, of course, poor chap. Funnily enough I'm not angry with him. It's as though we're both in it together. We said we'd meet soon. After all, it's a bit rough — one minute he's won a wife from her husband, and the next minute she's killed herself. He kept saying he was sorry. Funny how everyone says that, as though somehow it's everyone's fault.'

'She didn't mention someone called Stephen Maugham to you ever, did she?'

'No, I don't think so. Why?'

'It's nothing important,' said Jennifer, getting up to make him some more tea.

She opened the back door to let the tabby cat out into the garden and saw that it was raining lightly onto the long grass. During the months of her affair, Sheila had allowed the lawn and the flowerbeds to run wild.

'She said that she loved us both. But that's impossible, don't you think?' he said, as Jennifer closed the door on the garden. 'She said it was tearing her apart. She begged me to let her return. That was only last night on the phone and yet it seems like so long ago.' He picked up the black cat. 'Already I'm finding it hard to remember her face.'

16

Jennifer watched Tim's hand stroking the black cat over and over again as they sat in silence listening to the rain, which was heavy now and beating against the darkening windows.

'Could I make a phone call?' asked Jennifer. 'My mother's had an operation today.'

'Of course. Of course,' he murmured, his eyes closed like the half-asleep cat.

She walked up the stairs and the stairs creaked and she saw the dirt on the pictures, on the cord carpet, she felt the atmosphere of decay. Supposing Stephen Maugham had been here? Supposing he had in some way forced Sheila to take the whisky and the pills? She could almost feel his presence here, amused, cruel, lecherous as he made her die.

In the drawing room the phone was off the hook. Jennifer remembered that Sheila had always been very proud of this room with its bright turquoise walls and polished wood floors. She could hear the roar of the thunder in the distance.

Jennifer dialled her father's number. 'What news?'

'Good news,' replied Edward. 'The growth has been contained. The operation went well.'

So Lily had been right after all, thought Jennifer, with a rush of joy at her mother's victory, and a sudden sense of hope.

'She'll be out of hospital in two or three weeks and she's coming here for a few days so we can have a celebration then, all three of us together.'

Jennifer heard voices in the hall and realised that Tim's parents must have arrived.

'She's only staying a few days,' he continued, 'Not longer.'

'Of course, Edward,' said Jennifer, knowing that Sarah would stay exactly as long as she wanted.

Jennifer stepped into the hall, where a beaky-nosed woman with grey hair and a portly man were standing by Tim, who was looking very young and lost.

She said goodbye to Tim and the Humphreys.

As she walked in the rain down the street she was overwhelmed with a sudden bewildering love. It was an extraordinary sensation and for a moment she was so choked by its intensity she had to stop. She sat down, feeling faint, on the low brick wall in front of one of the houses. A passer-by stared at her anxiously, as though she might be having a heart attack, which in a way she was. The love flooded through her and she smiled at the stout man who quickly crossed the road.

All her concern with herself was disappearing as she sat staring in front of her, envisaging all the people she had met and would meet during the course of her life as passengers on a cruise ship to oblivion. She realised they were all on the same cruise, floating in the same direction, suffering the same storms of grief and sickness, and provided with the same choice of pleasures.

She looked up to the grey skies and enjoyed the feel of the rain running down her face.

Previously she had seen herself as a lone figure — like the heroines of her biographies, isolated, odd figures who rebelled against the normal pattern of things. But now she knew that there were more similarities than differences between her and other people.

After what seemed an hour but was in fact only a few minutes she returned to her house and wandered from room to room taking in each corner, each shadow, like a photographer taking shots of every angle and mood.

The shock of Sheila's death seemed to have given Jennifer back her life. It had jostled her into a new pattern, she felt. It was as though Sheila had saved her and now Jennifer was judging her own life, weighing up attachment to self and to others and working out what it all amounted to. And she knew, looking back now on her life, that what in the end mattered, what she remembered, were the people she had loved and the memories of affection and forgiveness. And she was lucky, unlike Sheila, to have another chance, to be able to live again, as her mother had another chance.

In the study, for the first time in a long while, she sat down and listened to some music without fidgeting or thinking about Martin. As she listened to Dvorak she felt the sadness and the glory of being alive, the grace and the splendour and the beauty in the dark waving trees outside.

She had escaped death this time. Suicide, or murder, or fate — whatever or whoever had killed Sheila, just a few doors down the road — had chosen that door that day and not hers. Sheila's had been marked with a cross, and she, Jennifer Hamilton, had been saved. She wondered if Stephen Maugham had perhaps called at her door before Sheila's when she was out, comforting her father. Or perhaps he'd been lurking outside when Richard had visited her last night. Perhaps he had been the face at the van window. But maybe all that was in her imagination. Perhaps there was no horror outside, only the horror inside, inside her brain, inside Sheila's, inside Richard's.

The next day she phoned Richard and he sounded nervous. When she said she wanted to see him, his voice changed and the sudden excitement in its tone matched her excitement at the thought of seeing him that evening.

'Let's get out of here,' he said, as he stood at the door. 'I don't want a repeat of Wednesday night.'

'Sorry about that,' she muttered.

'I'm sorry too. I . . . well, I overreacted. Actually I rang you later on. But you were out.' He made the statement sound like a question.

'With a girlfriend, as a matter of fact,' she said.

In the car she told him what had happened to Sheila, and he was at once silent and withdrawn.

'You don't really think Stephen Maugham could have had anything to do with it?' she asked.

131

'I thought we weren't going to have a repeat of Wednesday,' he growled, changing gear so abruptly she jerked forward in her seat.

'I suppose he could have forced her to take the pills and the drink,' she said quietly. He ran his fingers through his hair. He was ruffled, disordered.

'We'll never know, will we?'

'Why not? Perhaps we should go to the police.'

'You have no evidence, Jennifer.'

'Well, you seem to know a great deal about it.'

'I am not going to the police. Leave it be. She's dead.'

She watched his grave face.

'Stop looking at me like that,' he said. 'Forget it all. Get yourself back together again and you'll be safe from them.'

'Is that all that's important, being safe?'

'It is when you're not safe.'

She sat back in her seat.

'And you, do you feel safe?' she said after a while.

'I have never felt safe,' he replied.

'Richard, where were you brought up?'

'In Bexhill.'

'In Bexhill?' She found herself smiling.

'That's right. I was brought up by my mother and my grandmother, chiefly my grandmother, in Bexhill, by the seaside.'

'That must have been fun.'

'It wasn't at all. It was miserable. Fortunately I spent most of my time at boarding school.'

'Have you always been as depressed as you seem now?'

He glanced at her sharply.

'You seem very locked up in yourself,' she continued.

'I'm an only child, perhaps that's why,' he said tersely.

'That's not a reason. What is it, Richard? What's the matter?'

'Your friend died.'

'You never met her. Are you lonely, Richard, is that what it is?'

He turned his intense grey eyes on her.

She looked away. 'Where was your father?' she muttered.

'He left my mother for a younger woman. Usual story.'

'What does he do?'

'He's a barrister.' He paused. 'Jenny, are you all right?'

She swallowed and a great weariness overcame her. 'I suppose I am. I suppose I feel very relieved to be alive.'

'That's a perfectly normal reaction.'

'And anyway,' she said, 'I haven't quite taken it in. I can't quite understand it's happened. I still think I'll see Sheila again, at the shops perhaps. I can't comprehend that I won't.'

They drove on, through London, trapped in their own private thoughts.

'Martin hasn't crossed my mind recently,' she said as they passed the Gothic monstrosity of St Pancras, 'so I suppose that's something. And my mother, it looks as though she might be okay. Not that I ever really thought she wouldn't. It's odd that, isn't it, the things one knows?'

'Only when they turn out to be right,' he said, as he went through a red light.

She turned round anxiously, but there was no police car following them.

'Sorry,' he said. 'I was distracted.'

'You're always distracted,' she said, softly.

'I'm sorry. I don't want to be.'

'I can't imagine you at your desk in the Home Office.'

'Oh, I'm good at pretending. We're all good at putting on fronts,' he said. 'Civil servants manage to assume the appearance of normality while they're actually at work or going to work. They travel on the tube, have coffee at regular times, manage to send out all their letters — but inside most of us are cracking up.' He glanced in his mirror and took a sharp left turn. He was rather a bad driver, decided Jennifer, and put on her seat belt. 'They hope that if they keep up the appearance convincingly they'll grow into it,' he continued, 'that they'll become the appearance and every-thing will be fine. At work I seem a normal enough chap. I get in at nine-thirty. My secretary has no complaints. I wear the right clothes, behave in the appropriate manner, never turn up with

133

muddy shoes or a running nose or terror in my eyes. Things don't go wrong under my command, believe it or not. Or rather at work things don't go wrong. The rest of the time things go wrong constantly. But then I can assure you that, if it weren't for convention and routine, the corridors of the Civil Service as well as a great many other places would sound like a lunatic asylum. I need my solid job, very badly. Only very stable people can afford not to have sensible jobs.'

It was beginning to rain. He switched on the windscreen wipers. She felt very close to him.

'Other people don't see you like this, you know. Estelle doesn't,' she said.

'Estelle thinks everyone's wonderful. It's one of her most endearing qualities.'

'That's not true, as a matter of fact. She doesn't see everyone as wonderful.'

'Look, I don't know why you're trying to give me a morale boost. You're the one who's supposed to be in a state. I didn't even know Sheila.'

'Thanks,' she said, and her eyes prickled with tears. She felt a fool. She hated him.

His hand took hers. 'You're sweet,' he said in a blurred voice. A sense of relief filled Jennifer's body as they held hands tightly. His hand was extraordinarily warm.

They drove in silence through Islington and into Canonbury, past big dreaming houses. He parked and they walked together along the New River Walk.

Birds hopped around cheerfully and she could hear drops of rain falling from the huge trees, which floated peacefully in the early evening air, as if they were under water. Some music drifted from an open window and his hand was in hers and she felt curiously content.

'It's one of my favourite spots, this,' he said.

A pure white duck glided by and she smiled at the pomposity of its bearing. She saw one mallard peck at another mallard while the female duck they were quarrelling over sat on the water smug and dowdy in her brown uniform. Jennifer leant down to smell a rose. Beads of rain were scattered over its pink texture, glinting in the early evening sunlight like crystals. On the wet earth at the bottom of the rose bush she saw a snail trekking its way across its tiny universe, up and over stones, down valleys of earth, its black head sticking nervously out of its round frail shell. She touched a petal of the rose and her heart expanded so much with sadness and with love that it seemed too big for her body. It was pressing at her ribcage, trying to get out.

Standing here with Richard she had a sense of hope — hope not just for her own personal destiny, but for mankind, which was part of this majestic filigree of tree and leaf and stone. Three days ago, in Holland Park, she had longed to melt into the ground in order no longer to exist; now she would have liked to have sat down on the wet grass like a child and picked daisies just to get even closer to the sheer pleasure of being alive.

She thought again of her mother and her proud, defiant face.

The park gardener touched his cap as he passed the couple who were standing hand in hand.

A stray black dog shook himself as he entered the gardens.

'Get out,' yelled the gardener.

Richard and Jennifer walked along without speaking, over the bridge, past willows, staring at the backs of grand houses and at the huddles of ducks on the banks, some with their heads tucked into their wings, some watchful, some squabbling. She loved Richard along with everything else but not any more than anything else, she told herself. She was not in love with Richard. How could she be? She loved Martin. His hand was very hot in hers. She would have liked to have kissed him, in the same way that she would like to have kissed that baby, or the pompous white duck, or the rose with its soft-textured leaves. As they walked back along the way they had come, she decided that she did want to kiss him very much indeed. At that moment, he turned to her and bent his head. They kissed under a tree which dropped rain onto their heads, but they hardly noticed because they were so involved in that long, delicious kiss which went on and on until it seemed that they had always been kissing and always would be. Usually Jennifer became fed up with kisses after a short while. This one was so interesting and exhilarating and made her feel so extraordinary that she didn't want it to stop. Still kissing, they sat down on the park bench and continued like a courting couple, while Jennifer thought vaguely that there was really nothing at all nicer in the whole world than a kiss that went on and on and became more wonderful as it continued, as time withdrew, and place, and who one was and who one would be and wanted to be, a kiss which denied that there was anything important in the world beside kissing and being kissed and having his tongue in your mouth and his lips on your lips and your limbs and body hardly existing, or rather existing only as an extension of that mouth with all its passion and tenderness and the changing patterns of hot and cold as he traced his desire for you inside your mouth and with his hands as they pressed you close to him and you knew that with him kissing you you were completely happy and fulfilled except that you also wanted him to take off your clothes and lay you down at once.

17

Back in the car they kissed more, and he caressed her lips with his tongue and searched out the crevices of her ear while his hands were unbuttoning her shirt and his touch was firm, and very tender. He murmured her name as she kissed his neck. His skin was burning and her mind was swooning from the smell of him. His hand felt inside her shirt and he pulled out one breast from her bra and played with her nipple. He licked the finger which had been on her nipple and when it returned the wet touch made her brain cancel out as desire rippled through every inch of her body. His eyes were on her, watching her face dissolving, watching her breast, watching his hand gently moving up her leg, past her knee, under her thin crumpled skirt.

All around them the car was misting up but still anyone passing by could have looked in and seen the entangled bodies. But she wasn't thinking about that as his hand ran up her stocking to her suspenders and kneaded her there, on the warm top of her thighs, enjoying the different textures of the rough stocking and the soft skin.

'I want you,' he said in a throttled voice.

Their noses rubbed together and their eyes met in a longing gaze, which was more passionate than during the most passionate love scene she had ever had with Martin.

'We'd better get home,' he murmured.

She had a hand on his leg and his thigh was very strong. It was like metal. His lips touched hers and again an electric shock sent her mind reeling. His tongue was in her mouth, deep in her mouth, searching down into her open mouth while all the while the heat of his skin seeped into her nostrils and made her forget everything but him.

Just their lips were touching now, gently, teasingly, then he drew away from her.

'We must go,' he said, and she couldn't bear the distance between them, those few inches making her separate from him and the fire which was trying to mould them together. His hair was wild and his eyes disordered, desperate, full of desire. His chiselled face with its grey eyebrows and long nose contrasted with the life in his longing eyes.

He started up the engine and she pushed her breast back into the cup of her bra. As she did up the buttons of her shirt, she watched his every movement — his hand on the gear stick, his foot on the accelerator, his glance into the mirror. She nestled her face up to his, kissing his neck, burrowing her hand into his dry grey hair, his poor grey hair, his poor darling grey hair. His hand rested on her knee. She let her skirt remain pulled up to just below her hips because she wanted him to go on touching her, to caress the tender skin of her inner thigh, or at least to glance at her legs, as he was doing now with an expression of something which was almost pain.

The journey across London to Notting Hill was long, like a journey to another country. There were traffic lights and one-way systems. Too many streets and cars keeping her body at a few inches from him. She couldn't stand all the buildings getting in the way, keeping him from her aching body — while he looked straight ahead, his face serious, as though it wasn't really happening, as though his hand wasn't burning into her leg, as though her hand wasn't touching the warm flesh of his cheek.

His hand was on her right suspender and undoing it, slowly, expertly, pulling down the stocking, pinching her skin. She closed her eyes and concentrated on the pleasure, blacking out the rest of the world, blacking out thought, memory, concentrating only on his touch.

'Take down the other one,' he said, and she did, as he watched.

'That's better,' he said. His hand felt between her legs and she

138

thought again what a long way it was from Islington to Notting Hill.

When they stopped at traffic lights she wondered if other motorists could see in, see what his hands were doing, wondered if the men who were gazing at her knew why her face was flushed and her hair all messed up. She didn't care if they did.

She could see his erection making a bulge in his corduroy trousers. They were beige trousers. She had never thought beige an especially sexy colour until now.

The top three buttons of his shirt were undone, and she supposed she must have undone them. She could see the hairs of his chest.

Streets, houses, turnings, the distance and the yearning, the wonderful agonising yearning until at last they arrived at their destination. For a moment she felt shy. They were here. She put her stockings in her handbag and tried to tidy her hair.

'Come on,' he said.

She grappled in her handbag for some lipstick and then thought, damn it, opened the door and bustled out. With his arm around her shoulder they hurried to his house. As he unlocked the door she remembered how her aunt could never find her keys when unlocking the door of this same house, now a quite different door decked in smart brown paint and a brass knocker.

Inside he didn't switch on the light, although it was getting dark. He leant back on the door and looked at her, as if assessing her. She was blushing.

'I want to remember you like this, blushing, your hair all messed up, your face so beautiful. I don't think you know how beautiful your face is, you know.'

He put out his arms and she sank into them and he pressed her skin to the coarse skin of his face as his hands quickly undid the buttons of her shirt and undid her bra so that it fell to the ground and her round breasts were bare.

'Oh, my darling,' he whispered in a tone of awe and suddenly they were both on the floor, on the scratchy cord carpet, his trousers half off, her skirt pulled up, and he was making her scream

139

with ecstasy as he pushed himself into her again and again, pushing her against the rough carpet, making her come again and again.

Afterwards they held each other tightly and he kissed her desperately as though he were afraid of losing her.

'Are you hungry?' he said, after a while.

'Mmmm,' she replied.

They dressed and went out and bought champagne and take-away Chinese food, which they ate staring into each other's eyes, fingers sticky with the sauce from spare ribs, plates messy with rice, mouths cleaned out by the fresh taste of champagne, the rims of their glasses greasy from dirty lips. They pushed aside the plates and Richard leant over and kissed her across the table, smelling of sweet and sour pork with an aftertaste of champagne. They held hands as they kissed and the touch of his flesh again sent shivers through her body. They kissed for a long, long time until he moved round to her side of the table and, still holding her hands, took her with him onto the floor where he caressed her fully clothed, until she was desperate for him to unbutton her shirt, desperate to feel him licking her nipples, feeling her breasts, skin against skin, desperate for the exquisite teasing pleasure of his kisses on her neck, in her ear, on her lips, to penetrate again hard into her whole body. She wanted him to kiss her belly, she wanted him to tell her again she was beautiful, she wanted her soft skin to become softer, more yielding, she wanted all the misery and the fear to go as his body loved hers again with the passion and strength she had always known was there beneath the politeness and the secrecy and all those ordinary things which hid the extraordinary person under-neath who took off her clothes with such gentleness it made her cry and made love to her with such passion and love that she found it impossible to believe that this perfect happiness could ever end because it seemed more important than anything else, more important than plays or books or history, stronger than time or death, more full of love than anything and yet full too of a terrible sadness because Richard would grow old as she would grow old, because nothing was immortal although these moments together seemed immortal and took her beyond pain and beyond happiness. Afterwards she couldn't stop crying. He wrapped her in his arms and carried her up to the bedroom, where he made love to her again, as she cried, and they fell asleep in each other's arms, and Jennifer didn't really want ever to wake up.

She woke up with a start.

She saw Sheila's bewildered face in her mind's eye.

It had rained heavily during the night, but the new day was warm; the morning sun filtered through the thin curtains onto the bed and dappled the carpet. Jennifer felt guilty for having turned Sheila's death for love into her own happiness. She had been dancing on her grave.

She whispered, 'Good morning,' into Richard's ear and he murmured and turned and drew her close to him and began to kiss her and she let herself be kissed and gave way to the gentle ecstasy of his body rocking against hers. The love was a positive force, protecting her from the blackness climbing up the window.

'I do adore you, Jenny,' he said afterwards, relaxed, smiling, all that tension and misery gone. 'I won't let anything happen to you. You know, I think I admire every bit of you from top to toe. I adore those gorgeous shapely sexy legs of yours, and that wonderful warm furry place they lead up to. And I love that sensational bottom of yours and your hour-glass waist. And your arms are lovely too, and those slender long fingers at the end of them, and your neck, your elegant swan's neck, and then your face like a wicked elf. That's the best bit.' He kissed her on the mouth, tenderly. 'Your face is the best bit of all.'

She smiled into the loving eyes. But all the time something else was tugging at her — her anxiety about Sheila's death — so that she hardly listened to what he had said.

'I think I'd better go and see Lily today,' she said.

'What?'

'Lily, Mrs Maugham's friend.'

'I know who Lily is,' he snapped, the love replaced once more by dark grey, by shadows and storms. 'Why on earth do you want to see her?'

141

'I thought she might know something about Stephen Maugham's relationship with Sheila, that's all.'

He put his arm round her. It seemed they were clinging to each other on a raft in a stormy sea, embracing on the edge of a cliff.

'Well, I thought we might go to the Cotswolds today, and have lunch. Or a picnic. You're mad to want to see Lily. You must keep away from them. Really, Jennifer. I know what I'm talking about. Don't go.'

'I have to go. The shop where she works is in Victoria, and then I must visit my mother.' She smiled and he didn't return the smile. All the tension and unhappiness was back in his face.

'Don't you see,' she pleaded, 'I have to find out what happened to Sheila or I'll be guilty about it for the rest of my life?'

He let go of her, and turned away, his shoulders weary.

'Okay,' he said in a heavy voice. 'I'll see you back here later. There's a spare set of keys on the table by the door. Take them.'

She hurried along to the bus stop, disturbed as she recalled the weight of his shoulders. As she waited, the old fear of impermanence crept into her and she closed her eyes for a moment and wished. 'Let me remember,' she wished. 'Please let me always remember the good times. Let me remember lying with Richard in bed this morning with his arms around me. Let me remember the warmth of his kiss. Let me please remember the touch of his flesh. Don't take all these from me. I must keep them fresh. I must treasure them all, every memory of happiness. I must polish them like silver, keep them free from the dust of time and despair. So many have slipped from me. So many years no longer exist for me. Please don't let the colours — the colours of his eyes, that dark green pillow, the shades of his skin — please don't let them fade.'

When Jennifer eventually found the right chemist's shop in Victoria — after visiting each one she came to — Lily was standing behind the counter, solemnly, wearing a white coat. She was handing a customer his prescription with a thin smile.

Jennifer pretended to be interested in the soaps, the talcum powders, the sponges, and then became interested in the eye-shadows.

142

Lily was talking to the elderly customer for a long time. When he left, his head down, ploughing through the space in front of him, Jennifer went over to the counter carrying a bronze eyeshadow.

'I'll have this please,' she said to Lily.

'Hello, Jennifer,' said Lily flatly. 'It's Lily. From Mrs Maugham's.'

Jennifer's face cleared. 'Why, hello. I didn't see you there. What a surprise!'

'Been doing some shopping, have you?'

'That's right.'

Lily looked at her watch. 'Do you want a cup of coffee?'

'That would be nice. If you could spare the time.'

Jennifer paid for the eyeshadow, Lily put it in a bag then went through a door at the back and re-emerged a few minutes later in a coat which was far too big for her. She had given her hair a brush and smeared on some pale pink lipstick which made her even more cadaverous.

'It's quite warm out,' said Jennifer. 'You probably won't need the coat.'

'I always wear this coat,' explained Lily.

Jennifer noticed that, unlike most women, Lily did not glance at the enticing shop windows crammed with cashmere cardigans, chic little dresses, stylish hats. She directed her eyes straight ahead of her. One or two passers-by stared at her. Her legs were terribly thin.

They sat in a coffee bar and Lily ordered the coffees in her usual monotone. She asked for a large chocolate eclair for herself.

'Nothing for me,' said Jennifer to the waitress.

Lily did not take off her coat and Jennifer thought again what a sad little thing she was, so trapped somehow.

'It's a long journey up here from Surrey, isn't it?' said Jennifer chattily.

'Not too bad,' said Lily in her sepulchral voice. 'I like working in town.'

'Do you ever stay up in London?'

'Sometimes,' she said. 'I stay at Mrs Maugham's usually. It's a big house. Sometimes Stephen's there, sometimes he isn't. I go to the church from there. It's just round the corner. You see, ever since I was a small child, spirits have come to see me. They talked to me when my father was leaving my mother for the first time and they told me they would always be with me. They've kept their word. They told me there was no such thing as death. And that's true too. What passes for death is only something to make us appreciate life, to give it intensity. Death is only another kind of birth.'

'I hope you're right. What kind of spirits are they? What do they look like?'

'Like ordinary people,' she replied. 'There's an old man and a young child of, oh, about twelve. They come to me. We talk about this and that.'

'It must be nice having spirit people like that to talk to.'

'It is sometimes. But sometimes it's hard. Between you and me, I'm not sure they always give the best advice. One's too old, the other too young. I am becoming nervous of them. But when I'm lonely they come to me. And I am often lonely.'

Lily was sifting the brown sugar with her spoon.

'What do your spirits talk to you about?' questioned Jennifer.

'This and that. Sometimes they're very wise. Mrs Maugham says I talk to them too much. She says I talk too much in general. They died before I was born. They're happy where they are. It's very quiet there.'

'Do they ever ask you to do anything you think you can't bring yourself to?'

'Oh yes.'

'What kind of thing do they ask you?'

Lily looked away.

'This and that.' A rim of white coffee covered her upper lip. 'The little boy is the worst. When I refuse to do what he wants he sulks and vanishes. And I do like the little boy's company. He has a sweet face, with lovely green eyes, a bit like yours. But the old man is far nicer. He's very kind and he loves people.

The poor thing fell off a chair while changing a light bulb.'

Lily pushed her cup and saucer away. 'So I'm stuck with them really. I can't live without them.' She lifted up her eclair with both hands and sunk her teeth into it. A blob of cream fell onto her chin. 'And sometimes I find myself hating them. I hate the hold they have over me, the way they make me do things. Mrs Maugham has one too.'

'What hold does she have?'

'She's been very kind to me, like a mother, and I have come to appreciate kindness. My own mother shouts and screams all the time, that's when she's not reading romantic novels. Once I told her about my spirit friends and she said I should be put away. Mrs Maugham is not like that. She's understanding. She knows what it's like to speak to the dead. She's had the gift since she was a child. Her parents passed away when she was just sixteen, in that very house. The next year she was married to a very rich man she met at a ballroom-dancing class. She used to be very beautiful, you see. And she's clever, you know, very clever. She claims it's important to be able to communicate with the dead and the living. She speaks with your aunt, you know, and her husband, all the people she has helped onto the Other Side.'

'What do you mean?' asked Jennifer, as a coldness entered her body.

'Just that she's very understanding,' replied Lily, with the look of a weasel, 'when people are in trouble.' She reached for her cup and took another sip of coffee. 'And so their spirits assist her, or some of them do. They've helped to make her a very powerful medium. She's famous, you know. People have heard of her even in America. She says she wants me to follow in her footsteps when she passes over, that she'll be my spirit guide from the Other Side and help me to continue her work. But I don't know.'

The white dome of Lily's forehead furrowed.

'Sometimes I am troubled by what happens,' she said.

'By Stephen Maugham?'

'By him, yes, but by her too. She says that, if I break away from her, my old man and little boy will go too. And I can't imagine life without them. They've always been there, you see. Everything else has come and gone. And they'll always be there in the future too. When I die I'll be with them. I'll be with them for ever. They can be very comforting, especially the old man. He tells me always to have hope. Not like Stephen. He has no hope.'

'Tell me... Lily... do you think Stephen Maugham's a good man?'

'No,' said Lily. 'He's not at all good. I'd... I'd advise you to keep away from him. He has something. A kind of energy. But it's not goodness.'

'Does he frighten you?'

'Yes, sometimes. Mrs Maugham does too. Keep away from them both, Jennifer.'

Lily's face was drawn and serious.

'I can't do that, I'm afraid. You see, I want to know... do you think Stephen could have had anything at all to do with the suicide of my friend Sheila?'

'Oh yes,' said Lily very quietly. 'I'm sure he could. But don't let that worry you. It's nothing to do with you. You need have nothing to do with them again. Leave them alone. Leave them all alone.'

She looked round nervously, took a final bite of her eclair and wiped her fingers on her red paper napkin. 'I'd better go now.'

18

At the hospital, Sarah was sitting up in bed, haggard, as Jennifer entered. There was a young man in the room with Sarah. He was lounging in his chair, legs stretched before him, a stubble of beard on his chin and a languid expression in his eyes.

'Jenny, this is Frank, one of my most faithful hotel guests. He's a journalist.'

'How do you do?' said Jennifer severely.

'Frank has just come back from the Galapagos Islands. He's always adventuring somewhere exotic. Peru, the Amazon jungle, all over the place.'

He stood up lazily, shook her hand, and pulled up another chair beside the bed.

'The last time I saw Frank was about five or so weeks ago, just after I'd been told I had cancer. He gave me a wonderful book about destroying cancer with one's mind. Didn't you, darling? It seems to have worked so far.'

'With the help of an operation,' drawled Frank.

Sarah had applied too much blusher and too much foundation, so that she resembled the aged Elizabeth I. From her hands and face Jennifer knew how skinny Sarah's arms must be. They were well covered in a pink satin bedjacket. She wore her hair down, presumably to cover as much as possible of her face.

'The book explains how I must picture my tumour being overcome by the body's defences. It says one must mobilise resistance to the disease by enlisting the imagination — cowboys destroying Indians, white huskies killing a snake, that kind of thing. At first I visualised my tumour as another, younger, more

147

attractive woman flirting with a man I cared about, but that made me so furious it didn't do any good. Next I imagined the tumour as a difficult guest who caused trouble at my hotel by complaining and criticising. I imagined me as the body's defences sweeping down on him as he sat in the drawing room whining on about why there was no copy of *Golfing Monthly* among the magazines. I swept down on him with my chef and my housekeeper and told him to leave at once. It was such fun! I imagined him in all kinds of guises, in all different parts of the hotel, but always he is loathsome and he whines. It really is most amusing!'

'If all this has anything to do with the mind, I have no doubt you'll pull through,' said Frank. 'I know you. You've been ambushed by a disease, it's been lying in wait for you, and you are going to fight it off with your usual hope, faith and vigour.'

At that point Mike, the male nurse, entered slyly, like a scavenger, his long nose leading the way, with some pills and a glass of water. Frank was watching him with an expression of puzzlement. When Mike met Frank's eyes, he frowned and then quickly lowered his glance. He muttered to Sarah something about taking the pills and then scurried out, leaving Jennifer with a sinking of the heart.

'He's an awful young man,' said Sarah in a low voice. 'He keeps telling me it's hopeless to use the mind to fight disease. He's so defeatist. And it says in the book that the body sometimes uses cancer as a weapon to commit unconscious suicide. With nurses like him around, no wonder so many people die in hospital.'

'If I were you, I'd take no notice of Mike. He's very peculiar,' said Jennifer. She was staring towards the door through which Mike had gone.

'He certainly is. Do you know, he told me that doctors and nurses allow far more people to die in hospital than anyone will ever know? He said that, between him and me, some people couldn't bear their bodies disintegrating and asked for special injections. He looked at me with loathing as he said this. I told him that they must all be crazy. Personally, I wouldn't ask to die in a million years, whatever happened.'

148

'I've met him somewhere. I can't think where,' said Frank.

'Probably one of your low haunts,' said Sarah.

'Probably,' said Frank, looking away.

'Perhaps he's not like you. Perhaps he hates women,' said Sarah. 'Especially ill ones.'

She sank back on her pillows for a second and then she smiled, her old spirit rallying once more, resilient, optimistic.

Frank stretched out and patted Sarah's hand. 'You look your usual splendid self,' he said. He leant forward and kissed her hand, his eyes lifted towards her.

'I must be going. Now, Sarah, take it quietly.'

He ambled out of the room, in waistcoat and jeans and shirt with rolled-up sleeves, blowing them both a kiss in a sad imitation of something — of gaiety or campness or a debonair filmstar.

'Poor Frank,' said Sarah after he had gone. 'He's such a darling. Women are always falling in love with him and he with them but sexually he's only interested in men. He says he travels to get away from himself and is always surprised to find that wherever he goes he's still there making himself miserable.'

She turned and plumped up her pillows. 'So how are you, Jennifer? Are things getting better?'

'A bit. Except a friend, a girl about my age, committed suicide two days ago.'

'Oh Christ,' said Sarah, closing her eyes for a moment and shaking her head. 'How terrible. Over some man, I suppose. Women always kill themselves over men.'

'She was in love with two men — her husband and her lover — and couldn't bear it, I think.'

Sarah shook her head again. 'Foolish girl. She should have kept her lover secret.'

'Oh, mummy, honestly.'

Sarah's mouth was twitching until she smiled, and then suddenly she began to cough. 'I'm fine. Don't worry,' she said, and coughed some more.

'I'm tiring you. I'd better go,' said Jennifer, getting up.

'Don't. I like you being here. Sit down, please. Listen to me. I've

149

been thinking about you and I want to give you some advice.' She took her pills. 'Painkillers,' she explained sheepishly. 'Now look, just remember that, whatever else you might think, change is good for you. Don't try to play safe just because you're scared now. Think of yourself as a map that needs colouring in. As things happen, you discover more about yourself, the blank areas are filled in. You are only at the beginning of it all. You'll be amazed.' She smiled wistfully. 'Absolutely amazed at the variations of love you'll experience and how you'll be changed by them. You've hibernated with Martin for far too long. You should get out in the world and start living. You know all about the mind, you've been a success, you should learn about passion. There's much more to you than you think. You should discover it all, every bit of life. You shouldn't be afraid.'

'I know what you're saying. It's what you always say. But it's only half true. You know as well as I do that sometimes it's important to play safe, that life can be threatening. It is important to take care. Only the very strong can be free like you.'

'Jennifer, you really must . . .' and Sarah began to cough.

'Look, you're exhausted. You really must sleep. Shall I stay with you?'

'No, you might as well go now, darling. I suppose I had better get some rest,' she said wearily. 'How boring it is to be ill.'

They kissed each other goodbye.

Outside the door, Jennifer closed her eyes for a moment and prayed that her mother would recover. She opened her eyes. At the far end of the corridor, standing by the window, looking straight at her, was Mike. There were trolleys and other nurses between them, but for a moment everything stopped and there was just that watching figure in a white uniform.

Jennifer closed her mother's door behind her and wished she could lock it. She hurried to the lift. It took a long time to come. Eventually she gave up and ran down the stairs, brushing against nurses and doctors and people with strange, wasted faces and bodies they dragged up those stairs as if wishing they could lose them.

The drab walls, the memory of all those beds upstairs, crowded in on her. She wanted to be as far as possible from the needles and the drugs and the operating table with its knives.

She ran out of the main doors of the hospital. Outside, her panic was still with her. She looked one way and then the other expecting to see the white figure of Mike at the end of every pavement. She couldn't remember which way to go. She thought she was going to cry as she stood there in confusion. She turned right and hurried across the car park towards the tube, as it began to rain.

And then it happened.

In the distance, over on the far side of the car park, she saw a disorderly man with a hand raised, waving. She knew he would have been waiting whichever way she turned.

'Do you want a lift?' yelled Stephen Maugham.

She forced herself to go on walking towards the white-haired figure and his battered van. He was wearing a donkey jacket and baggy jeans, more like an odd-job man than the salesman he was.

It was this van she had seen the night before Sheila's death.

'Yes,' she said as she drew closer. 'Yes, please. There's something I want to talk to you about.'

His waxen face was smiling at her, distorted into shiny folds around those black pinpoint eyes.

She turned and looked up at the fourth-floor window of the tall modern hospital where Mike had been standing. She knew he was there now, watching.

She climbed into the van. The back was strewn with teddy bears and dolls and soft toys wrapped in polythene bags. She remembered her interview with the social worker surrounded by toys. That seemed a long time ago, when the horror had been contained inside her.

'How are you, my dear?' said Stephen Maugham.

A sweet wrapper and an old copy of the *Daily Mirror* lay on the rubber mat at her feet.

'Not too bad,' she said. She wondered why she was sitting here with this man she feared in this desolate hospital car park, the rain on the windows obscuring the outside world, enclosing her.

151

'I've just been visiting a friend of mine,' he said. 'Terrible pity. Heart attack.'

'My mother's in there. Your friend Mike is looking after her.'

He nodded, neither confirming that he knew this, nor denying it.

She took a deep breath. 'Did you know that Sheila Humphreys committed suicide?'

'Ah yes. I called in on her shop and somebody told me. Such a pity. Such a lovely girl. We had lunch just a day or so ago.'

'I know you did. Was there anything she said which made you think she was suicidal?'

He offered her a cigarette. She shook her head. His hands were stained with nicotine and his nails full of dirt.

'Oh yes. She was very depressed. She said she longed for the peace of death. She wanted to stop being tired, she said.'

The rain hit at the roof and dribbled down the windscreen.

Jennifer did up her safety belt. 'I live in Fulham, as perhaps you know. We'd better go there if that's where we're going.'

'Why should I know that?' he said, smirking.

'You were there Wednesday night, outside my house.'

'I wasn't, my dear. Your clever little mind is playing tricks on you, I'm afraid.'

It was then that she knew she should get out of the car. She should offer some neat excuse, open the door and escape from the threat in this unhappy man's voice. But she couldn't. It seemed necessary to her that she complete what she had started. She wanted to know what would happen next. She wanted to know exactly what had happened to Sheila. She felt responsible and yet oddly irresponsible too, as if she had stepped into Stephen Maugham's car against her own free will.

He started the car and they drove off. As they drove, he chatted about his friend's heart attack, and then about how people whose lives temporarily stopped on the operating table spoke of being outside of or separated from their bodies. He said these people who clinically died, albeit briefly, had a sense of great comfort and even bliss.

'Mr Maugham . . .' said Jennifer decisively.

'Do call me Stephen.'

'Mr Maugham. Sheila's suicide was horrible. It was sordid as everything evil is sordid. She smelt of whisky.' Jennifer was holding her handbag close to her as though it could protect her. The windscreen wipers smashed from side to side.

He smiled to himself and took another drag of his cigarette, letting the ash fall onto his trousers. He coughed. 'You've thought about it a lot, haven't you, my dear? You've thought about it seriously. The thing is when you're dead it no longer matters what people think, whether it looks sordid or glorious. People don't kill themselves for effect.'

'It does matter,' she said, sitting up straight. 'What about her husband, can you imagine how he feels?'

'From what she said, he sounded a pretty weak person. He deserves to suffer.'

'Who are you to say that?'

He ran his tongue over his rubbery lips. There was dandruff on the shoulders of his donkey jacket.

The streets they were passing were a long way away from them, in another world. Gleaming black streets, the swish of cars, only last night she had been in a car with Richard, full of desire, dressed in the same thin skirt, the same black blouse. Always in transit, it seemed to her, taken to destinations by other people, controlled by other people, out of control herself.

'Surely even I can express an opinion? I know I'm not one of your intellectual middle-class friends, but at least I can express an opinion, don't you think? Or perhaps because I'm just a salesman you think I don't have the right. Is that what you think?' His voice was suddenly rough.

'No, of course not.'

'I don't even make much money.' He coughed again. 'My wives left me a little, but not much. So perhaps that's it. I'm a salesman who doesn't make any money, and so you despise me.'

'I do not despise you.'

He lit another cigarette. The ashtray was spilling over.

'The children like the toys. I like children, although I have never had any myself. They're much nicer than adults, I find. On the whole I find that adults avoid people like me, people who lack social graces. They're friendly to my sister, of course, because she is quite genteel in her way, don't you find? She can be very charming.'

'I wanted to talk to you about Sheila,' insisted Jennifer.

'I'm boring you, am I, my dear? I am sorry. What do you want to say about Sheila?'

'I want to know how she died.' I'm being brave, thought Jennifer. Or am I? What is it I really want from this old man with the big hands who smells of death, of nicotine and stale clothes? Why is it I am drawn to the Maughams, away from the love which only yesterday seemed to fill my whole soul?

'Don't you know? I'm afraid I don't. I didn't ask the gruesome details when I went into her smart little toy shop and found all the little shopgirls there in tears. I didn't think that would have been very tactful, do you?'

'She died of pills and whisky.' If this rattling old van crashed now, would I really care? It will happen to me another day, another year, oblivion, the letting go. I would never see Martin again. But do I care? He's a stranger now. My death would not even be of much consequence to him. She tried to remember the love and sense of hope which had almost obliterated her yesterday. But with Stephen Maugham beside her, she found there was only fear and distrust.

'Pills and whisky. How very sad,' drawled Stephen. 'And what else do you want to say, my dear? Are you going to say you don't understand how she could do a thing like that? But that wouldn't be true, would it, you know quite well? Sometimes you have longed to pass over, to have all the sorrow removed for ever, to have a good long sleep, because you get tired too, don't you, my dear? I expect you're more puzzled by why you have to go on living. It's that you find puzzling, not the other thing...'

All these journeys of her life, all taking her nowhere in particular. Tube stations, railway stations, people all eager to get somewhere. And yet in the end there was nowhere to go. Stephen Maugham was right. There was only the rain outside and people

154

trapped in trains, in cars, in buildings, in hospital beds, waiting for something to happen.

'But I know you've talked to my dear sister about all this. She tells me everything you know, we're very close, my sister and I, but I don't always tell her everything because I don't trust her. Marjorie has a very forceful personality — as, no doubt, being an intelligent girl, you have observed. She's my older sister and she can, I have to admit, be a little dominating at times. Personally I think I'd have been better off without her. Are you shocked? It's a terrible thing to say, I know, but you see my sister has rather taken over my life. She runs it. She says I'd be nothing without her, and of course she's right, quite right, perhaps.' Jennifer could hear the struggle in Stephen Maugham's voice, the struggle to speak properly, to appear to be a calm, sensible, educated person, when all the while the blackness was sucking him down. 'She even gives me money because as you know her husband was very wealthy, very classy he was, a successful businessman, you know. And some of her clients give her money for helping them, usually in their wills — "to further the cause" you know.'

She quite liked listening to his voice as he tried to keep it steady, to stifle the roughness and the anger which kept flaring up. It had a rhythm to which her own confusion responded.

'Now tell me, my dear, am I going the right way?'

'Oh yes,' she murmured, 'absolutely the right way. It's the next turning to the left.'

The car drew up outside her house.

'And how is your mother, my dear?'

'Not well,' said Jennifer. 'But she's very tough, very self-reliant. I think she'll be okay.'

'Maybe,' he said, in a way which suggested she wouldn't.

He was watching her intently, his eyes roaming over her.

'I won't ask you in,' she said. 'I'm in a bit of a hurry. I've just got to change out of these clothes.'

'Just a cup of tea, surely?' he said. 'You could offer me a cup of tea after I've brought you all this way. That would be only polite, I would have thought.'

155

He stubbed out his cigarette and smiled at her.

'I'm sorry, but if you don't mind, I'd rather not.' But she was sitting quite still, not making a move to get out.

'You don't want a salesman in your house, I suppose. I can understand that. Only it seems a little hard on me when I've come all this way. And anyway, I have to make a phone call. I'm late, you see, for my next appointment, because of taking you home.'

For a moment she was sorry for him, for this strange old man who wanted to enter her house. What did it matter? She had accepted his lift, after all.

'Okay. Come in. But just to make the call.'

He followed her to the door and stood close to her. Why am I letting him in? What do I want from him?

She switched on the lights and hurried briskly into the kitchen.

He made his call from the white phone in the kitchen, watching her all the while as she went through the motions of tidying up, getting on with things, being busy and preoccupied.

'No reply,' he said. 'They must have gone out.' He looked out of the window. 'What a day, isn't it? What terrible weather. I couldn't sleep last night because of the rain.'

She put a plate into the washing-up bowl, marched over to the table and started to clear up the rest of the knives and forks and dirty mugs she had left there for days.

Stephen Maugham pulled out a chair and sat down. 'Just one cup of tea, and then I'll go.'

She opened the cupboard doors and seized two tea bags from the nearly empty box. She shoved them in mugs, switched on the kettle, and leant back against the cupboard.

He smiled at her. 'Dear me. You are in a state, aren't you?'

One hand rested on the table, the other held a cigarette. He had an air of relaxation and amusement, as though he were perfectly happy where he was, and wasn't budging.

She plonked a mug in front of him.

'Sit down, my dear,' he murmured. 'Relax. After all, you did invite me in.'

Jennifer wished Richard were about to arrive. She wished

she had arranged to meet Richard here, instead of at his house.

'I said sit down,' he repeated, and she found herself sitting down.

He smoked as they sipped their tea, her lipstick marking her mug, his eyes on the stain her lips had left.

The wind was swishing through the trees, shaking the house with giant hands, rattling the windows. A terrible lethargy spread through Jennifer's body, all the vigour of a moment ago quite gone, as Stephen Maugham moved his chair closer to the table, closer to her.

'My dear, you pretend you're not, but really you're very depressed, aren't you?'

'I'm fine,' she said wearily. 'Just a little worried about my mother.'

'You're not fine, my dear. That just isn't true. Your life has gone the wrong way. A wrong turning or two and you've ended up somewhere far worse than just a dead end.'

'Actually, I'm perfectly okay,' said Jennifer in a false voice. 'Although I admit I wasn't a few days ago, even the last time I saw you. But I wanted to talk to you about Sheila, not about me.' She was surprised at how difficult it was to form these words with Stephen Maugham's eyes on her. 'I wanted to know how she died.'

'Sheila? But we've discussed that, haven't we, my dear? All I know is that she got to the light, she freed the spirit. What does it matter how she died? Things are much nicer over there. A foolish girl like that would have had a miserable life and caused other people endless trouble. One moment in love with one person, the next another.'

'You are quite wrong about her. Her unhappiness was temporary.'

'And yours? Do you think your unhappiness is temporary?'

'I told you. I'm not unhappy any more.'

Stephen Maugham's thumb was running up and down the handle of one of the knives left on the table. There was something almost sensual about the movement, as though he were caressing the knife.

'Jennifer, tell me, my dear,' he said, leaning so close to her that she saw the open pores of his shiny skin. 'You're a very sexually attractive girl. Do you have a boyfriend?'

'Yes, I do, as a matter of fact.'

'A new boyfriend?'

'That's right.'

'And is he a decent person, worthy of your . . . love?' He said the word 'love' as though he could have chosen any number of less attractive words.

'Yes, he is a decent person.'

'And his name, is it by any chance Richard Stevenson?'

'That's right.'

'We have had dealings with Mr Richard Stevenson in the past, you know, my sister and I.'

'Mr Maugham, I really don't want to hear what you have to say.'

'But my dear, this is important. You see, Richard Stevenson is an unsavoury character.'

'Please. I don't want to know anything against him.'

She forced herself to stand up. He lit another cigarette and took a long drag.

'Sit down,' he said, and his hypnotic eyes were fixed on her. She sat down.

'You mustn't trust him, my dear,' insisted Stephen Maugham. 'You mustn't grow dependent on him or he'll treat you as he treated his wife. I have to tell you the truth in case this happens.'

He stretched out his hand for hers. For a moment it lay over hers and it was cold like stone. A shudder went through her and she took away her hand.

'Poor Jennifer. I'm afraid you shouldn't see him again, my dear.'

'Why?'

'He is . . . unreliable.'

Stephen Maugham dropped ash into his half-empty mug of tea.

'What I have to say will shock you.'

Stephen Maugham showed his yellow teeth as he smiled.

'Mr Maugham, I don't want to hear what you're going to say.'

There was a long silence. Even the rain had stopped.

'Please go away,' said Jennifer in a low voice.

Stephen Maugham stayed where he was, dragging on his cigarette, one elbow on the table, watching her intently.

Jennifer's hands were shaking.

Suddenly he grinned and dropped his cigarette into the mug of tea in front of him.

'I don't even need to say it, do I, my dear?' he said, standing up. Suddenly he was big, confident, victorious.

He grinned again, his eyes disappearing into the folds of his skin.

Jennifer was trembling all over.

'I'll no doubt see you later, at my sister's,' he said, brushing down his jacket as though her house had dirtied it. He lumbered out of the room. She heard the front door close behind him.

Jennifer sat in shock at the table, staring at the mug Stephen Maugham had left behind, floating with ash and a darkening, wet cigarette end.

She decided to go over to Richard's. She wanted to find out if what she feared was true. She tried to stand up, but her legs were made of jelly.

Later, when she had recovered, she took a taxi to Richard's. As she journeyed, the spare keys to his house in her pocket, she thought back on his behaviour since she had met him: his moodiness, his temper which often seemed on the brink of erupting into violence, his obsession with his dead wife, his remarks about guilt and the importance of confession. And she remembered his anger when she said she was visiting Mrs Maugham.

She let herself into the dark house and as she did so she recalled the image in her mind whenever she was close to Richard, of opening a door into a house full of shadows. All was silent except for the slow tick of the grandfather clock. She stood in the hall, looking up at the stairs from which that girl, Richard's wife Cynthia, had fallen. How dark it was in this house, and how still.

'Richard!' she shouted. 'Richard, are you there?'

But there was no answer. There was a door to the right, a door to the left, a passage leading down into the kitchen, the staircase leading upwards, a series of choices which filled her with unease.

She wished she had asked the taxi to wait for her.

She found herself walking up the stairs. She passed herself in a mirror and her eyes had an extraordinary brightness.

How eerie it was here in this half-decorated house, with its bare floors and its air of abandonment. She walked into the bedroom where they had made love the night before and smelt his warm, male smell, so much more pungent and alive than that of Martin.

She turned away and climbed to the top floor. Once, in her Aunt Stella's time, this house had been full of life, cats, dust, scraps of paper holding her aunt's scribbled notes, empty bottles of wine shoved behind broken armchairs. And now the house was held in time, unfinished, unresolved, caught in the past, the moment when the girl with the red hair and freckles had died. It was as though she were still mistress in the house. Her torpor, her inability to get anything done, her dislike of the rambling old place, were all still here, waiting, watching, affecting Jennifer, infecting her.

A board creaked behind Jennifer as she crossed the upstairs landing, but she knew there was nothing there, only the draughts under the boards and the ghosts of the future and the past trying to get into her mind. She opened the half-painted door in front of her and entered a small room with flowery wallpaper and a big white wardrobe. On the kidney-shaped dressing table, beside a silver brush and comb, was a photograph frame containing the face of the girl with ginger hair.

Jennifer took a step back.

The girl was smiling, but there was som thing desolate in her smile, as though she saw no love and no point in anything and never had.

For some time Jennifer remained hunched up on the floor of the attic room with her hands over her ears to drown the sound of Cynthia's sudden cries as Richard pushed her down the stairs.

19

Jennifer went straight over to Estelle's, where she sat in virtual silence while Estelle talked. There was already one bottle of wine empty at Estelle's side, and another half empty. The manuscript she was reading was splashed with red wine. It was a cold, damp evening, almost like a dawn.

'Extraordinary really,' Estelle was saying, 'that men are so beastly and contemptuous about women when we have the greatest gift of all — an endless ability to love. I even loved Sheila, you know. I suppose it's because we're built to have lots of children and to love them all.' She poured herself another glass, the wine from the bottom shedding a drip onto her bright green tracksuit.

Jennifer asked to sleep on Estelle's sofa that night. Her hostess staggered off to bed early, and Jennifer knew that it was grief for Sheila, not self-pity, which had made Estelle rambling, depressed and drunk.

Jennifer lay awake staring up at the crack in the ceiling. She felt very empty inside and worthless. The wonderful, warm man who had loved her so was a murderer, someone who lived in misery because he refused to acknowledge his guilt. As for her mother and father, she hadn't encouraged them to get back together when she should have, long ago. She had wanted her father to herself. She hadn't saved Sheila. She had been selfish with Martin and had deserved her punishment. But she had thought she could put her own lands in order, with the help of Richard's love and, most of all, his need for her. His need had reached some deep part of her which had not been touched before. It had penetrated her selfishness, struck some hidden well of feeling and love which could have

161

changed her for ever. But now she saw that Richard's love was a figment, a charade like the rest of her life. He had needed comforting perhaps. He had wanted to dissuade her from finding out from the Maughams what really happened, certainly. She had been used. But how could that be true, when she loved him, when he came towards her with all the world's love in his eyes?

She lit one of Estelle's cigarettes and nearly choked on it, but it gave her a buzz as she sucked, drawing in the nicotine which flooded through her body and made her suddenly peaceful and certain of what she wanted to do.

She left the flat quietly, without waking Estelle.

Soon Stephen Maugham was grinning at her, showing his yellow teeth, a cigarette in his hand.

'Come in,' he said, taking her arm firmly.

He led her through the dank hall into the drawing room with its heavy curtains closed. 'We've been expecting you,' he said, and slipped his arm around her. She didn't shake it off.

As she stood smiling at the grey figures in the semi-darkness of that museum-like room she thought of her childhood hero, the poet Shelley. He was half in love with death, like the rest of them, those doomed Romantic poets and lovers, Chatterton, Keats, Byron. She imagined their death masks facing her on the top of the bookshelves by the curtain, all looking at her, glorious in death, ending their lives in drama, rejecting the slow ebb of age.

She wished the living people in the room did not look so dead too.

Oddly enough, today Stephen Maugham seemed to have much more life in him than Mrs Maugham. With his arm round her, she was close to a strong power, a source of life and death.

He took away his arm and Jennifer felt smaller, sadder, less magnificent.

Mrs Maugham was sitting on the sofa swamped by a smile. Her knees were plonked far apart and the light cotton dress showed the thickness of her thighs.

Beside her on the sofa, very close to her, was Lily, stick-like in her white overall from the chemist's shop. Her skin was

162

unnaturally pale, like marble, unreal. She smiled at Jennifer.

By the grandfather clock stood the boy Mike with those bleak eyes and thin, hardly human lips. He too wore white — white trousers, white shirt done right up to the neck, very starched. She decided that he had no heart at all. She knew he'd had it all scooped out at birth as Mrs Maugham's husband had scooped out the insides of the dead animals which crept round the room and watched her from the mantelpiece. He had a sneer in his eyes and in his mouth. She knew that he enjoyed destruction because there was nothing else at all which stirred any feelings in him.

'My dear,' said Mrs Maugham, getting up. 'How delightful! We were expecting you. But you're a little late.'

Jennifer looked at her watch. It was nearly midnight.

'Now, you haven't told anyone you were coming here, have you, my dear?' asked Mrs Maugham solicitously.

Jennifer shook her head.

Stephen Maugham touched her arm. She smelt his staleness. Mrs Maugham sat down again. She reached for a chocolate from the box on the small rosewood table beside her which held the only lamp in the room. It had a pink shade, the same colour as the ribbon on the corner of the chocolate-box lid.

'My goodness, Lily, do get Jenny a glass of brandy. She looks quite ill.'

Lily brushed Mrs Maugham gently on the knee as she rose to her feet.

'Why don't you sit down, my dear?' said Mrs Maugham to Jennifer.

'I'd rather stand.'

Mrs Maugham's left hand searched for another chocolate as she put her slippered feet on the embroidered footstool. 'Now, my dear,' she said, 'we all came here today to have a talk about you and with you, to give you one last chance. There has been considerable discussion. Myself and Lily ...' Lily handed Jennifer a glass, all the time watching her with those sad grey eyes. 'Myself and Lily,' continued Mrs Maugham, 'we want to ask you again to join our little group. I suspect you know all about it by now.' In the pause she popped a sweet into her mouth and appeared to gulp it down whole. 'My goodness! It wouldn't surprise me at all if you had come broadly to the correct conclusions about our aims and methods. You are an intelligent girl and a pretty one and I like you. We would welcome you if you wished to join — in spite of Mike and Stephen's protests. Personally, I never take all that much notice of men. Do we, dear?' she said to Lily. 'Now, Jenny, what do you say?'

Jennifer shook her head. 'I don't know what you're talking about.'

'Oh, come now,' said Mrs Maugham. 'You really know. You're as psychic as the rest of us. You don't need it all spelled out.'

Mrs Maugham's face stared into hers. Jennifer turned her gaze away onto the hummingbird in the glass case: how peaceful the bird was, far away from all these people who embodied the horror and emptiness from which she longed to escape.

'But why?' she murmured. 'That's what I want to know. Why do you all want to do it?'

'Different reasons, my dear. Each one of us has different reasons. There are always different reasons for everything people do. They might sometimes give them the same name but they are different, always different.'

Jennifer took a sip of the brandy. For a moment she wished the rug on which she was standing would rise up and carry her away, far away from this claustrophobic room, away from these twisted faces with their shiny skins, away from humanity which plotted and schemed and killed. Here, only the animals seemed innocent, and look what men had done to them: disembowelled them, turned them into ornaments.

'Why do *you* do it, Mrs Maugham?'

Mrs Maugham screwed up her face, as though thinking hard. 'In part for pleasure, I suppose. It's something to do. And I have to admit that I enjoy power. Perhaps I should have run a big company.' Mrs Maugham scanned all the faces in the room but no one even acknowledged her joke. For the first time, Jennifer sensed that they all hated Mrs Maugham. 'Also, my chosen ones usually want to pass over. They are grateful to me and they become my helpers on the Other Side. They give me information, provide me with material to impress people at seances and meetings.'

'That's horrible.' Jennifer's limbs were made of stone. She was unable to move. They were all staring at her, a statue in a gallery.

'Not to me, my dear,' said Mrs Maugham. 'And remember they want to pass over. I help tired souls make their exit.'

Lily's hands were clasped on her thin knees, knuckles white as her face. There were shadows under her eyes.

'And Lily,' said Jennifer. 'Why do you do it?'

'My voices,' she said in her flat little voice. Her knees were clamped tightly together as though they wished to compress themselves out of existence. Lily was taking up as little space in the world as she possibly could, in contrast to the fat woman in the splodgy orange and red dress who expanded over the sofa like a jellyfish melting in the sun. 'My voices tell me that these people are suffering and in pain, although they don't realise this until I convince them. I can recognise them the moment they enter the shop. They drag their feet, their eyes are dead, they're nervous. They come in with prescriptions from their doctors. But they're not suffering from illnesses. They're suffering from their whole lives. I befriend them — usually they're lonely — and then I visit them in their homes.'

Mike was fiddling with a button on his shirt as he fixed his fish eyes upon Jennifer. His pointed features stabbed into her like daggers and his voice was spiteful. 'I encourage the sick to die because they should be dead. They shouldn't be allowed to pollute the world with their coughing and their slow dying. Usually I smother them with plastic bags.' He moved truculently from foot to foot, as though daring her to criticise him. 'Sometimes I inject the soles of their feet with insulin. The coroner never finds out because the patients are riddled with disease anyhow. In the eyes of the world they die of cancer, bronchitis, or whatever.'

'But that's murder.'

'Oh no,' he said, rubbing his pointed nose and blinking with sudden nervousness. 'I always make sure that they first say to me that they want to die. Anyway, all I do is obey Mrs Maugham.'

Jennifer saw her mother lying in bed while Mike walked softly towards the sleeping woman through the dark hospital room.

'Your mother won't come to any harm,' interrupted Lily coolly. 'I made Mike promise me that.'

Jennifer was rocking slightly and thought her legs were about to give way.

Mrs Maugham crossed her arms disapprovingly.

'That promise was somewhat presumptuous, Mike,' she snapped.

Mike reddened and stared miserably at his shoes, which were rather old and scuffed. 'Sometimes I feel that I've had enough,' he murmured.

For a moment, Jennifer pitied him.

'I don't really know why I do it,' drawled Stephen, dropping his cigarette end on the floor and stepping on it quickly as if on a venomous spider. 'Except that my sister tells me to. And my sister has always told me what to do. Marjorie has always controlled my life, you know.'

'What a liar you are, my dear,' said Mrs Maugham lightly.

The room was very still. As if arrested in mid-movement, the stoat, the fighting cocks, the bison's head, stared at burly Stephen lighting another cigarette; at Mike, still uncomfortable; at Lily, all skinny arms and legs, sitting so tensely; and at Mrs Maugham, heavy hands lying on heavy limbs, face impassive. The animals observed, unchanging, unchanged, while the human beings were locked in private fears and hatreds in the half-light of this tomb.

'Even as a child, Stephen was a terrible liar, you know. Once they found him out, all the other children used to tease him about it. He was such a pathetic little boy, you have no idea. But I protected him, of course, because he was my brother. And now he's grown up into a rather pathetic man, a drunkard and a lecher. How ashamed our poor mother and father would have been of him. Luckily, I married well and have always been able to provide him with money.'

'Do not be so unkind,' said Lily, meeting the eyes of Stephen.

166

'Unkind! My dear, I didn't know you cared about him. I'll have to put a stop to that, certainly. And I should be grateful if you would not speak out of turn, my dear. Otherwise I might have to arrange for you to see a mental doctor, and he would put you away, and you wouldn't like that, now would you, dear?'

'My mother always adored her, you know,' said Stephen. 'My mother died here, in this house. I would have been here but Marjorie said our mother didn't want to see me. My mother left everything to her.'

Jennifer's stomach tightened and she closed her eyes. She saw Mrs Maugham looming over an old woman. Mrs Maugham had a pillow in her hands and a smile of satisfaction on her face. It was a thinner face, uncushioned by the fat accumulated by years, and she could see its cruelty.

Night was forcing its black face against the windows.

'My wives all died,' mused Stephen. 'Odd, isn't it? Everyone I have ever cared for has died, and my sister has grown stronger and stronger.'

'Stephen, be quiet,' said Mrs Maugham firmly. 'You're not yourself tonight. Have another brandy, if that will calm your nerves. Although I suspect you've drunk quite enough this evening.'

Stephen flicked ash onto the floor.

'Now Jennifer,' said Mrs Maugham in the indulgent voice Jennifer herself used at school when addressing a good child after speaking to a naughty one. 'What do you say? Will you join us?'

Stephen was standing near to Jennifer and she could sense his hatred of his sister. There was someone else close to her too, the woman with the vengeful eyes and beautiful face.

'Will you join us?' repeated Mrs Maugham.

'Sorry?'

'Will you join us, my dear?' said Mrs Maugham with a touch of exasperation.

Jennifer's brow furrowed. She was swaying on her feet as if on a boat in a rough sea. There was sickness in her stomach. 'Oh no, why of course not. I couldn't do that. I am not that kind of person, you know.'

'It would be an excellent use of your powers,' said Mrs Maugham patiently. 'An attractive, bright girl with your will-power and psychic gifts could persuade anyone if you really wanted to. As a writer and teacher you have the contacts, the social prestige. And you could talk to some of the young girls at your school. Who knows? You might discover someone like Lily. Heavens! You have no idea how useful you could be to us! It would give your life a point and — as Lily so wisely said — relieve a great deal of misery. You really mustn't listen to what those men say. As for me,' she looked down shyly, 'I like to pretend that I'm harder than I am. As a matter of fact, at heart I see us having a mission to soothe mental and physical suffering by helping people to make their exits from life. Surely you can see the merit in that?'

'I don't want to join your group, Mrs Maugham,' said Jennifer. 'I have no intention of doing so, and never have had.'

Mrs Maugham became again the younger Mrs Maugham, squinting, hard. She was biting at her plump lips.

'You are quite sure you have no desire to join our group, or any of the other ones?'

'Other ones?'

'Oh yes. Oh yes, my dear. Our organisations are everywhere. In chemist's shops, in church halls, in hospitals. The kind old lady who befriends the widowed old man. The family doctor. The do-gooding middle-aged lady without children, only the light of goodness in her eyes.' She laughed. 'They're all in it. Heavens, my dear. They're all over the world. Medicine tries to take away death. We put it back. We encourage people to take their deaths into their own hands. The end crowns all. Who wants to die by mistake or ignominiously? Suicide is a noble end. It's a very assertive, positive way to go. Are you sure you won't help us in our work?'

'Absolutely certain. Surely you know why I have come here?'

There was a moment's silence and in the silence Jennifer could

168

hear the hum of her blue bird's wings. It was the tiniest, most delicate creature in the whole room and yet at times it seemed huge, dazzling, a fairytale dream in blues shut into its dusty glass case. Beady eyes, upturned tail, all ready to move on, to take its jewelled, shimmering body elsewhere.

'Yes, my dear, I do know,' said Mrs Maugham.

'But I would like to see Richard once before I died.'

'Richard? My dear, that isn't possible.'

'But he needs me,' she said. She saw those grey, aching eyes and felt weak with longing.

'My dear, Richard's no good for you. He didn't help you regain your sense of reality. Why, he's even stranger than you are! No, you have understood that you don't belong here on the earth plane any more. Some people live with that knowledge for years but don't have your courage. Come and sit with us, my dear.'

Before she could stop them, Jennifer's legs obeyed the voice's command and she came to sit beside the fat lady who snuggled up close. 'There, there,' Mrs Maugham said. 'You must not see Richard. This sense of unreality you have won't fade, you know. You had it even before your parents broke up, didn't you now? And their separation made it worse. How can you continue to live in this way? You can't invest ordinary things with significance as other people can. As for other people, you don't really even like them, do you? You don't feel comfortable with them. You're always longing to be home in your room with a book. You have nothing, Jennifer. You're already a spirit wandering between the two worlds, and you know it perfectly well.'

Jennifer nodded.

'Now, isn't it comfortable here, on the sofa? That's what passing over will be like. The spirits tell me time and again. There's a light at the end of a long tunnel and when you arrive there you're free of your body and your anxieties and everything that keeps you in torment here, where you don't belong.'

Stephen Maugham was standing over them. He took a knife from his belt, underneath his donkey jacket.

Jennifer stared at the knife, which was glinting in the darkened

169

room. It had a wooden handle and a long steel blade. She looked up at Stephen Maugham into eyes full of death and felt sorry for him. He was fingering the knife. It was a kitchen knife, similar to the one he had been handling earlier, in her house.

'A gypsy called here earlier today,' said Stephen. 'He sat on the doorstep and sharpened the knife.'

Mrs Maugham squinted up at her brother. 'Put that away now, dear,' she said. 'Get yourself a nice drink.'

He took no notice.

Mrs Maugham turned back to Jennifer as though Stephen were just a naughty child. He stayed where he was playing with the knife, tossing it from one hand to the other.

'Now what was I saying?' said Mrs Maugham. 'Ah yes, I wanted to say that I envy you, my dear. Personally, I don't really like the bright lights and the glare of living one bit. I'd rather have peace. I know you've felt the same. When you're watching the television you're relieved not to be participating in the dramas. You just sit quietly, feeling things at second hand, like a ghost, like someone who has passed on. It's much less painful than taking part in it all. And my goodness, my body, it's beginning to go wrong . . . aches and pains and worries. I'd like to be free of it all. While you . . . you'll never grow old like the rest of us.' She glanced up at her brother. 'Stephen, put that knife away. We have sleeping pills for her.'

'I don't think we should give her the pills,' said Stephen.

'I think we should let her go,' said Lily in a clear voice.

'Get the sleeping pills, Lily,' said Mrs Maugham as though she hadn't heard.

'I'm afraid I'm not going to do that, Marjorie. I like Jennifer.'

'Get the pills.'

'I said that I won't, Marjorie.' Lily sat stiffly. In girlish pony tail, white overall and pinched little face, she looked too frail to stand up to Mrs Maugham, even with words.

'Do what I say.' She stuck her fat hand over Lily's arm, and Lily winced in pain but did not move.

'Leave Lily alone,' said Stephen.

170

'I will when you put that knife away,' she said.

Jennifer heard pealing laughter in her head. It was Cynthia's laughter and it sounded curiously fresh and happy.

'Mike, take that knife from Stephen.'

Mike shifted from foot to foot and eyed the knife with fear.

'I think I'd better go now,' he said. 'I have to go back to work, as a matter of fact.'

'You stay here,' roared Mrs Maugham.

Mike scowled at her. Grumpily, he pulled at his nose with his skeletal fingers and for a moment Jennifer thought he was about to take himself to pieces. It would not have surprised her much. Nothing had sense any more. She could have watched him take off his nose, his ears, his mouth, and only been a little perturbed. She wondered where Richard was. She wanted to see him just once more, just once more, she told herself, just once more she wanted to feel the heat of his lips on hers and hear the whisper of his voice in her soul.

'Give me that knife.' Mrs Maugham rose to her feet, a stout little figure. She was fidgeting with the pearls around her neck, and there was sweat on her forehead. What a great deal of make-up she wears, thought Jennifer, as though she wants to disguise herself completely: thick yellow foundation and orange lips.

Sister and brother faced each other. He did not take a step back, and she did not take a step forward.

'Give it to me,' she said, holding out her hand, all her will concentrated on Stephen.

'It's no good,' said Stephen. 'That girl is back again. She is standing between us. You have no power to make me do what I don't want to do.'

'What girl?'

'She haunts me, Marjorie.'

'What is it? What are you talking about?'

'The girl.'

'What girl?'

'You shouldn't have killed her.'

'That's right, you shouldn't have,' said Lily.

'Tell me what girl you are talking about.'

'The beautiful one. Cynthia Stevenson.'

Mrs Maugham's shoulders relaxed. 'Don't you remember? She fell downstairs. Her husband pushed her. We provided him with an alibi. You're confused, dear, you've drunk too much.'

'I've drunk nothing.'

'Just give me the knife, and then you can take Jennifer home if you like and give her the pills yourself, and some whisky. You'd like that, wouldn't you, dear? And the rest of the bottle of whisky you can have for yourself.'

'That's what you made me do to the other one. And now she haunts me. And I made that other girl die, little Sheila, because she looked like Cynthia, because I wanted to rid myself of Cynthia.'

'Well, that must be very distressing for you, my dear. Now don't be childish. Give me the knife.'

Stephen was shaking, and there was a tremble in his voice.

'It was you who killed them, not me. Without you, I'm nothing. You've told me that many times. And I want to be nothing. I want to be the feeble ordinary man you say I am.'

'Look here, Stephen, nobody killed the girl. She killed herself. I happened to be visiting her at the time. She lurched out of the room and threw herself at her husband. She stank of drink and he pushed her away, and she fell. That's all. He had just come back from work. He didn't know what to do. He was determined to go to the police about what he'd done and I persuaded him not to. I said he'd go to prison and lose his job. In fact I feared he'd tell them his suspicions about us, about you. I saved you, Stephen, because you're my brother, because I love you.'

'You saved yourself,' he said.

'I do love you, Stephen. I have always looked after you, given you money. Don't you remember?' She took a step forward. 'Anyway, the girl Cynthia was an unpleasant little thing.'

Mrs Maugham's small fat hands were opening and closing nervously.

'You see no good anywhere, do you, Marjorie?' said Lily

blankly. 'And yet you should see Richard Stevenson's eyes now. He's thinking about Jennifer. They're full of love.'

'Lily is having one of her turns. Don't listen to her,' said Mrs Maugham. 'Sometimes I think you'd be better off in a mental hospital, Lily dear,' she said, still facing Stephen.

'Richard,' continued Lily steadfastly, 'is thinking about Jennifer ... but he's also thinking about the statement he made this afternoon, to the police. All that guilt which made him so wretched is clearing now.'

Mrs Maugham's body stiffened, and then she spun round. 'I'll kill him if he's done anything to us.'

'Well, he has. He told them what happened that night, and he told them everything he knows about you,' said Lily, with uncharacteristic relish.

'Where is he?'

'In a car, on his way here, to find Jennifer. He's driving very fast. He should be with us any minute.' Lily rose to her feet. 'Cynthia has gone, you know. I'm going now. It's all over.'

Jennifer's eyes were fixed on the hummingbird, which hovered in ecstasy in its glass dome, eternally sucking nectar from its flower. Its body's soft armour was a glory of colour, so perfect, far above the grey pavements, the cars, the women with children and with sorrow, the men with briefcases, all standing alone on the rock of their lives, the water lapping around them, washing away their years little by little as they called and waved to each other from across the dark expanses.

Jennifer pulled her hands up over her face, over her hair, sweeping back the cobwebs of despair.

Stephen continued to toss the knife from one hand to another.

Mrs Maugham was scarlet, her wig lopsided, malice and fear spread over her features.

Lily, Stephen and Mike were watching their former leader with such contempt that they hardly noticed as Jennifer made her way to the door, past the whimpering dog in the dark hall, and out of the house. She could hear Richard calling in her mind. She ran down the street.

173

The sky above was black, pinpointed by stars, and the air was soft on her face, like velvet. She felt suddenly, miraculously, happy.

Headlights shone onto her, dazzled her, and when she opened her eyes Richard was beside her. From now on, she thought as she flung her arms around him, I want bright, warm colours. I want no greys any more.

A few minutes later, by the light of a street lamp, Mike and Lily saw Jennifer and Richard lost in a hug which seemed to have gone on for ever. They stopped and stared and were even a little moved.

Oddly enough, Lily and Mike were not much moved by the news they received later that night — of Mrs Maugham's death. She had slit her wrists with a kitchen knife . . . or so the story went. At the time of the suicide . . . yes, of course, of course Stephen was with them, at dinner at a little Greek restaurant just off Notting Hill high street. Lily and Mike both felt glad to be free of her. Their reaction was shared by Stephen Maugham, who gave much of the money he inherited to charity, and died soon afterwards of drink.

In his will, Stephen left the hummingbird to Jennifer, who gave it as a wedding present to her parents when they remarried. Her mother hurled it at Edward one day, in a rage, and the glass dome broke, but not the hummingbird.

Abacus now offers an exciting range of quality titles by both established and new authors. All of the books in this series are available from:

Sphere Books,
Cash Sales Department,
P.O. Box 11,
Falmouth,
Cornwall TR10 9EN.

Alternatively you may fax your order to the above address. Fax No. 0326 376423.

Payments can be made as follows: Cheque, postal order (payable to Macdonald & Co (Publishers) Ltd) or by credit cards, Visa/Access. Do not send cash or currency. UK customers and B.F.P.O.: please send a cheque or postal order (no currency) and allow £1.00 for postage and packing for the first book, plus 50p for the second book, plus 30p for each additional book up to a maximum charge of £3.00 (7 books plus).

Overseas customers including Ireland, please allow £2.00 for postage and packing for the first book, plus £1.00 for the second book, plus 50p for each additional book.

NAME (Block Letters) ....

ADDRESS..

....

☐ I enclose my remittance for _____

☐ I wish to pay by Access/Visa Card

Number ☐☐☐☐☐☐☐☐☐☐☐☐☐☐☐☐☐☐☐

Card Expiry Date ☐☐☐☐